DIVA

DIVA

Living in the Fast Lane

Neil Vickers

First paperback edition
Ethan Fosse Publications
Ethan.fosse10@gmail.com

ISBN 978-1-80541-838-2 — paperback
ISBN 978-1-80541-837-5 — eBook

TABLE OF CONTENTS

CHAPTER 1

It was not a lavish upbringing, but my parents were always there for us. Whatever we needed, my father got for us. Living in Africa was a gift as we learned so much so fast. I was born into a large family with older sisters and brothers; I was the youngest in the family. My siblings were street wise; they had to be to survive the poverty in our village. Everybody worked for the good of the family, but although life was simple, it was a battle of wits as to whether you had a good meal.

Every day was different from the next; there was no plan. Everything was mapped out for the next day, but the next day was similar to the day before: a fight to eat a decent meal, a fight to find clothes to wear. We did not have the money to go to the local market to buy clothes, so we had to try and make our own out of clothes that had been thrown away by others.

I became an expert at sewing clothes and started to put my own mark on the clothes I made. I would sit there patching the clothes together, endless lines of cotton, day after day. I started making them to sell for myself, and then, later, I made clothes for my sisters and brothers. As we grew up, my older siblings were dating, some getting married, and they all seemed to follow the money.

Money was a commodity that was never available when we were young, so seeing my sisters and brothers doing so well was a good thing. Most of them lived with their partners on the island in Lagos -- yes, I grew up in Nigeria -- but we had moved beyond our humble beginnings. My siblings had bought my parents a nice house for us, and I looked after myself and my parents. I used to go to my sisters' houses on the island; it was a different world to the village. We were now in Lagos. It was a busy, dusty place sometimes, but this was my life, and I wanted the dream.

This was never going to be where I would live for the rest of my life. I wanted more; it was not in my destiny to remain in Lagos. I spent time with my siblings; my sisters all had a good lifestyle. I used to go to their houses and swim in the pools, and I would sneak up into their bedrooms and try on their designer clothes and shoes. I was already a diva. I even looked like a diva; I just hadn't earned the name, though it belonged to me. I was going to make sure I milked it to the max.

I would be leaving Africa and spreading my wings, but I was not of age and would have to obtain my permission from my parents to leave in search for a life I deserved after all the hard years spent growing up in Lagos. It was years of learning, and I learned so much. I had started creating my own clothes and designing them into fashionable garments that made people in the streets stop me and ask me where I bought them. When I said I had made them, they looked in disbelief at how this teenager could have the talent to make clothes that belonged on fashion models in New York, Paris, Milan, or London.

This was her moment to shine; she was using her sewing talent to progress her newfound career to another level. She was never going to be a seamstress, but she was beginning to know fashion and what it meant to all the people who followed fashion and style. It was a world market of all the best life could offer, and it would be her way out of Africa into the world of fashion. This is what she was about; she had a perfect figure, was beautiful, and had really good taste in fashion. She just needed the right break to take it to the next level.

In her mind, she was already there. Every thought involved fashion and style. It was her dream to be seen and to lead the way for the fashion of the future. Her thoughts were on tomorrow's fashion, today was now old and everything moves forward, and fashion in reverse to her was a step backwards. In her thoughts, she wanted to see fashion moving forward: new designs, new materials, new ideas -- she was a diva in the making. She would be instrumental in future fashion and just needed to be able to make that big break into Europe and America.

She had her sights set on being a global traveller and socialite. There would be no boundaries for her; every country needed her fashion input as far as she was concerned. They all needed her fashion sense to be bestowed on them. She wanted not to be sewing clothes but advising on the style and quality of the clothes design and producing. If she wasn't wearing their clothes, then they were not current in the market: only top designers would be welcome. She would be the one to set the standards for fashion. Everything she would wear would send a statement out to all the designers that they had to step up their designs to accommodate her. If she was not wearing your clothes, shoes, and handbags, you were not up there at the top of fashion designers. She was dreaming about the day she would leave Nigeria and start her career as a diva. There was no recognised qualification apart from having the looks and figure of a fashion house model and the know-how of being able to mix and match clothes, shoes, and bags to stand out in the crowd.

She had mapped out a route from Lagos, Nigeria, to Milan in Italy. That would be her starting point: to contact the fashion designers there and try to introduce herself into their marketing outlets as the socialite that would be recognised by all the large fashion designers like Louis Vuitton, Burberry, Jimmy Choo, Ralph Lauren, and Dior. She was so determined she would masquerade as a socialite that every fashion house would want her to endorse their latest designs.

She had to give herself two years to install herself firmly into the magazines of Vouge and Elle. She was desperate to leave Africa; she had served her time there. The world was her oyster, and she was going to chase the dream and everything that was luxurious. She was never going to be a full time African woman again. It was her birthplace, and she would always put her family first, but she had to open her eyes to the fact it was all out there in the world for her to take. She wanted it so bad.

CHAPTER 2

She could not fail; she would follow her dream and realise the rewards for the service she would provide moving amongst the rich and famous. In her mind, she had completely said goodbye to her younger life. She was nearly 18 and a woman with her own mind. She was not going to be second best, as a diva she was her own person, and she would be ruled by no-one but herself. She would be making the decisions, thinking all would not be acceptable, she needed to have positive answers to all her questions. She didn't have a negative thought anywhere in her body. Where she was bought up, negative was not a word used. Without being positive they, as a family, would have gone hungry.

They had to have a positive outlook in life or suffer. She only had three months to go before she was 18. The diva would soon be on her way into the unknown. Although she had lived her life dreaming about places she had never been, she was on a mission to go. She would be losing her African given name of Jabari, and she was now going to rename herself to match her celebrity lifestyle. At 18 she would be of age enough to make her follow her dream, making and sewing clothes was at its end. She had managed to secretly save some money for herself, which she called her slush fund and which she could access for her passport and flight out of the country into the land of opportunity she craved so much.

Africa had good memories, but she had her sights on making life decisions and being the best at what she did. There was no second best. She would never accept anything but number one in her category. That everything had to move forwards, onwards, and upwards was in her thinking already, and defeat would be devastation. She would never accept defeat; her mind had been made up years ago. She would never marry and have children in Africa; her future children would only have the best she could give them. She had eaten enough dust out of the village and heard enough car horns to last for the rest of her life. First class was the only option. Once she had the funds, she would never fly economy -- it was too lower class.

Her sights were set high on business and first class; she needed to have space if she was travelling. She referred to economy as baggage; she was now at another level -- baggage was not for her. She would choose her airline carefully. If they had no other options they wouldn't get her business. Once she had her status, upgrades to first class would be the norm and expected. A diva never uses her own money if she was traveling for a reason. Somebody else would be picking up her travel expenses.

Paying money for travel was not an option. Everywhere she was going was carefully planned to ensure all expenses were paid up front. There would be no credit extended to anybody; everything was chargeable at the going rate for the status she was portraying.

It was now three months until her 18th birthday and everything was in place. She had crossed every t and dotted every i. Twelve weeks, and the bird would fly the nest and be on her way. She had her whole life in front of her. She had everything to gain and nothing to lose as she had come from nowhere to be at a celebrity status. The diva was soon to be on her way to fame and fortune.

That time would soon come, but she had to get things in place. The passport, the visa, and the USA was her priority. She was going to do it all on the same day, although it would cost her more. Nobody would know in advance; on the day of leaving, her friend would witness the photograph. The timing of departure would be the same day; she was not going to wait a day longer. This young lady was chasing after her destiny; she would not be seeing Africa again for a few years. She was out to make her mark, nothing would get in the way, she was already in flight mode, and she could feel herself flying to Europe.

Milan, Italy, would be her home; she would make her name there and create new contacts and friends with benefits. If there were no benefits, they would not be on the friends list; nobody was having a free ride. If they wanted her company, they were going to pay for it: a diva doesn't work for nothing. Everything that came out of her mouth, good or bad, would have to be paid for. Advise on fashion would be an extra and payable up front, she had set her parameters, and she would not be moving an inch to accommodate anybody.

She had all the rules, and no one would break them; she was here to work. This was a fledgling business, and she was focused on taking it to the top. She was taking no freeloaders or prisoners; this she was adamant on. If they bought nothing to the table but themselves, they wouldn't be dining with her. She was ready to roll and that passport was long overdue; the visa would be on it, allowing her to stay and work in the Schengen countries of Europe.

She was never going to work as such. She was going to socialise with all the dignitaries, wherever they were, she was going to be there, mingling amongst them. She just needed a break to gain access to all her clients. She already had lists of who lived in what country and at what status they would have to be to interest her. She was not interested in armchair dreamers; she wanted successful men who could prove their worth. Nothing else would be acceptable in her mind; only a proven record would prompt a response. She was above the norm. The norm no longer existed in her world, as she was now on the road to becoming the best diva the world had ever encountered.

She had over 10,000 followers and friends on social media; she would be calling in some favours as she travelled. Her followers and friends would be providing accommodation in the short term; she had made the right friends in the places she wanted to be. This would be part of her access plan to fame and fortune. She had her own program; there would be no apprenticeship, as she had studied enough.

CHAPTER 3

She knew exactly what she wanted; nobody had the qualifications to teach her anything. She already knew it all. She would be their teacher in the future, obviously at a cost to the new ones coming up behind her. She would have to prove herself first. She was at the last night she would spend in Africa. In the morning, she would be catching the early flight to Milan, where they were ready for her. A shock would be arriving tomorrow; Milan should have been forewarned she was on her way.

As the morning light shone through the window, she knew it was her time to travel. All the travel documents were in place. This young woman was up and ready to go long before the rest of the family woke up. She crept around as not to wake anybody, as they would ask questions as to where she was going. She had written letters to all the family members; she had done individual ones to everyone. After all, she had been planning this for a long time. Well, virtually her whole life.

She had arranged the taxi to meet her down the road so as not to wake any family member. She took all the notes out of her bag and put them on the table. She had asked everybody to forgive her for the way she left as, if she had explained herself, she may have been persuaded to stay and marry in Africa and that was not what she wanted. She wanted the world to be hers; nobody would interrupt her goal of being the best.

She arrived early, and the taxi arrived five minutes later.

"You're late" she said to the taxi driver, "and I told you to bring a good car. I can't be getting out of this junk at the airport. Take me there straight away. I'm already late."

"Yes, ma'am," the taxi driver replied.

"Put your foot down and get me there," she said in a hurried voice. "Can't you go any faster, driver?" she said, tapping her hands on the back of his seat. "I'm in a hurry, step it up." She sat there glaring at him in the rear-view mirror, making him feel uncomfortable.

He had picked her in the next street to hers, which was an upgrade to hers. The driver made conversation.

"Your house is very nice, madam," he said.

"Don't mind my business," she said in a sharp voice, "mind your own and get on with the driving, get me to that airport fast."

She was wearing a short skirt with a matching jacket; it seemed her long legs went a long way up for such a short skirt. She had the best shaped legs; she could see him glancing through the rear-view mirror as she fidgeted around, taking one long leg across the other. She caught him looking as she moved.

"Never mind my legs," she said sharply. "Get on with getting me to that airport and keep your eyeballs in. I don't want you crashing the car."

"No, ma'am," he said.

"How far away are we?" she asked.

"Not far now, madam, just around the corner."

"Well, keep your eyes on the road, we don't want to end up in the airport check-in in this banger. That won't do my image any good. Do you know who I am?" she asked the driver.

"No," the taxi driver said.

She replied, "well, your boss will hear about you when I call him. If you had spent more time driving instead of looking at me, we could have been there by now and on the plane. It's not been a good experience for me, here," She said, handing a hundred dollar note over the seat to him.

"Give me all the change," she said.

"I'm sorry, madam," the taxi driver said to her. "I don't have change for that."

"What?" she said in an angry voice. "I was assured you would have change, give it back to me."

The taxi driver said, "it's fifteen dollars, madam."

She was sharp and said "It's not my fault you have no change. What kind of taxi are you running? Give me a pen and paper now and hurry, I'm late."

The taxi driver gave her a pen and paper.

"I want a receipt as well," she said. "And hurry, I'm late." She wrote a number on the paper.

"Here," she said, "phone the office at 9am and they will pay you cash."

"But," the driver said.

"Don't bother me. Come and open the door and take my cases to the check-in desk. Just call the office for payment at 9 o'clock and don't forget. I will call them to confirm the payment."

"Yes, madam" the driver said.

"Well, get off, then. You made me feel sick with your driving. It's a wonder I'm not reporting you for it."

"I'm sorry, madam," the driver said.

She walked away from him, putting her hand in the air to wave him off. Under her breath, she said, "goodbye, cloth head. Serves you right for coming into my life. Good luck with the payment, you fool." She had given him some non-descript office number. It would be lucky if it even rang a number. He had been taken to the cleaners by the best; she was never going to pay for anything.

She would not be paying today or any other day. She was a diva and everything was on a plate now. All she had to do was ensure her purse never saw daylight out of the handbag she put it in. She had checked in her case but was arguing with the man who said it was 10kg above the 23kg allowance.

She said, "are you stupid?" to the man. "Stop acting like a child. Put the bag through and don't ever talk to me like that again."

"Like what madam?"

"You know," she said, "put that case through now."

The man looked up. Her face was fierce like a lion. He looked at her and then the case -- she was too much to handle. He put the tag on the case and sent it on its way to the bagging area. She said, "at last," and turned and wiggled her bum at him as she made her way to the departure area and passport control.

She was messing about, holding up the queue, bringing attention to herself, just being a diva, expecting the porter to get a trolley and take her and her bags to passport control. She had checked in her case 10kg overweight, but the main bags she was carrying, they were all in designer bags: Gucci, Louis Vuitton, and Chanel. All fakes, of course, but under her breath she whispered to herself, "don't worry. They will all be real soon."

She would never be seen with fakes again once the money started to roll in. She was on a mission to be the best; she would not fall short.

"Come on, hurry up," she said to the porter. "Get me to passport control. I need to get into the executive lounges."

"Yes, ma'am," the porter replied in a husky, subservient squeak.

"Wait there in case I need you again," she said in a sharp voice.

"Yes," the porter replied. He was going nowhere with her beady eyes watching him.

She turned and said, "okay take off the bags and put them on the table, you can go now." She blurted this out in front of everybody.

"Yes ma'am," he said as she pressed a coin into his hand.

"Thank you," he said without looking down. She said, "my pleasure," as he walked off. She had put a bolt washer in his hand; he looked down at it as she scuttled through passport control. She was clear of the imbecile, as she called him while muttering to herself.

CHAPTER 4

She was as deadly as a viper; she could see him looking over with a dumbfounded face. He wouldn't be getting rich on what she gave him; it wouldn't buy him time, never mind anything else. She had done him out of his income. He was expecting more, but nothing was leaving her purse of any value, as it was all hers and not accessible to anybody but her. Penny washers were her preferred payment method; cash payments would not be the norm for her unless it led to more money being transacted into her account.

She wanted to build reserves, not spend them. He wasn't having more than she gave him, but everything was based on tips: there were no wages for staff, just what they picked up on tips. This time, he had drawn the short straw and gotten the diva. He wouldn't be spending the tip she gave him. It would be more useful on a bike wheel.

There would be no food in the cupboard for his family today, he would have to choose his clients more carefully and not go for the pretty ladies. They would always be the ones to take your money and run. There was no mercy with a woman like her. She was trying in her own mind to convince herself she was a nice person and anything she did would come back big time and vindicate her from her illicit practices.

She had a lot of these miscomprehensions that she was doing the right thing. But her take on it was that she was providing a service to social circles and, hopefully, social media would be the main goal to focus on. She had set out to meet as many people as she could see; her diary was full. She had managed somehow to get full names; telephone numbers and addresses for offices and even home addresses, in some cases.

Her plan was to obtain information of places near the addresses she had in her diary and meet the celebrity or other and strike up a conversation about her having lived in the same life in the same area as them. She would say she had moved to a completely different province but had come back to complete some business deals, the idea being for her to gain their trust and move into their circle of friends.

All the angles she would use had been meticulously worked out and four out of ten would have a good result. She had told herself that setting the parameters too high could lead to a catastrophic collapse of her future empire. She had seen greedy people fall and had learned from it. Her motto *was bait the line and wait for the fish to come to you.* If you go to the fish, it will see you coming and swim away.

The diva was precise in her strategy. She was the sprat to catch a mackerel; the diva had arrived. She just needed to board the plane and leave Africa for the foreseeable future. It had been good to her and taught her a lot of how the world worked. She had studied fashion, finance, business, and, most of all, people and how they would work in her favour.

She now had something in common with all of her contacts; all she had to do is read her notes on them. When she would meet them and befriend them, she would already have her stories in place: she was in a financial mess as her boyfriend stole all her money and assets and she had to flee Africa to save herself from her high-flying drug dealing boyfriend of three years.

Her age had just increased from 18 years old. She was now 22 years old to all the people she would be meeting.

She was looking for the young rich celebrities; they were in her target age group. They might have less knowledge about someone like herself, and they tended to have more parties and gatherings than the older celebrities. She was to be in the young scene like young Formula One drivers, tennis players, or footballers: they were all fair game for her.

Although she was Nigerian, her mother was Brazilian and her father was Nigerian, making her mixed race and lighter in colour. She was looking a million-dollar babe, she was so pretty, enough to win the crown of Miss Nigeria, but she knew that was only going to be a short-lived. She wasn't interested in the crown. She wanted the money she could master, as the diva was now a businesswoman. Everything was for sale, but the prices set would make a rich man's eyes pop out.

She had a minimum price, but the maximum would be based on their ability to pay for her company and to be seen with a diva. A top socialite nobody could compete with. She wouldn't think twice about destroying any competition that got in her way. She had indicated that she would buy drugs and plant them in a rival's bag and call the police and tell them the rival was trafficking drugs to get her away from her man, so the table would be clear for her to step in and take over as his new girlfriend.

She would be ruthless in her tactics to remove all the competition; she had set the bar so high she would be having trouble jumping it herself. Time was on her side. She was four years behind her stage age, as she was a performer, and she was the star of the stage.

CHAPTER 5

It was time to board the plane; she was seated in baggage, as she called it. This was not going to be good for her. How was she going to meet a wealthy person in baggage? She needed an upgrade to business at the least and first class at the best. She got to the entrance door of the plane and asked for the head stewardess or steward. They came to her.

"I'm ever so sorry," she said. "I always travel first class as I have a problem with my legs, and they are liable to form blood clots unless they are horizontal all the time or I'm standing. It restricts me so much in what I can do, and I will have to spend most of the flight standing. My new manager has booked the wrong ticket, and I'm in a dilemma. Could you see if you have a seat that will accommodate my needs? I'm so sorry to put this on you, as I know you're going to be busy with the passengers, and you might not be able to find something.

"I will take anything as long as I don't have to stand the whole flight to save my blood clotting. Thrombosis is terrible to have."

"You have to stay here," the stewardess said, "let me have a look." She left and went upstairs to business and first class. Then she came down and said, "come this way madam, I've managed to find you a seat."

"God bless you, you're so kind," she said going up the stairs. "You're a credit to this airline. I will ask my director to write about your excellent service. Thank you so much."

The stewardess said, "we have one in both classes, business and first. Would you like to choose?"

"Oh, first class every time, darling. I hope you don't mind."

"Not at all," the stewardess replied.

The diva said "yes, we all have our likes, and unfortunately I can't fly without them."

It beggared belief how she had conned her way into first class from a regular ticket, but she was a master at cons. She had learned from the best, herself, she was lying down on the seat smiling and laughing about how she had got the first-class seat. She had been thinking about her new name, as the African name was history.

In her mind, she had got the perfect name for herself. From now on, her name would be Madam Sazzar. She was ready to circulate around first-class passengers: here was the money. She had a certain target: rich people. She could tell their wealth by the clothes they wore, right down to the shoes and bags. She could tell the difference between a Chanel dress and a Valentino. She had a keen eye for fashion and styling.

It had been her passion to read fashion magazines; she knew that designers had their very own take on fashion styling. She knew any item of clothing from Gucci to Burberry from Louis Vuitton to Hermes. There was nothing hiding in fashion she did not know about; she could smell money as she walked around the first-class seats.

She found her first victim as she bent down putting her hand out.

"Hello there, I'm Madam Sazzar. Pleased to meet you, my fellow passenger."

"Oh, pleased to meet you, Madam Sazzar," the lady replied in a surprised voice. *Who was Madam Sazzar?* she thought.

The diva had made a grand entrance into the world of first-class.

"Good morning to you both," she said as she addressed the husband, looking over to examine his $80,000 gold Rolex.

"Excuse me one second, please." As she itched her hand, she was thinking about how she was going to relieve him of his watch. It was making the palms of her hand itch to think about it, as she bent over to shake his hand. You could see her breasts nestled into her tight-fitting, body-hugging dress, denoting her hourglass figure. As she stretched, the man on the opposite seat caught her eye. She had a split dress showing her legs. They went right the way up. His eyes followed the split skirt, and she gave him a wink as she continued to effectively flirt with the husband of the woman.

She apologised to the woman and said, "very sorry I nearly fell on you; I didn't get your name."

She said, "it's Gloria."

"What a fabulous name," the diva said.

Gloria said, "you too, your name is quite distinctive."

"Oh no," the diva said, "my mother was very careful not to call me a name that someone else had. My mother said she spent up to a year researching the name and there were no others with this name.

"I feel privileged to have the name Madam Sazzar, but I was thinking of changing it to something simpler. I've been very close to royalty in Africa. I'm very well connected. If you're ever coming back to Africa, I can take you to all the best places and introduce you to all the royal families in Africa."

"Yes, that would be so nice on our next trip for you to come and introduce us to your royal friends."

"Were you here on business, Gloria?" the diva asked.

"Yes, we are in commodities."

"Oh, I see. Can I ask what commodities you're in?"

"Oil and gas, dear," Gloria replied. The diva's head virtually fell of her shoulders; these were mega rich people. She needed their friendship. She could see the man looking and smiling opposite, and she nearly growled at him. This idiot could be instrumental in ruining the friendship she was hatching.

He looked like he had skanked his way into that seat, the deadbeat, he was no good for her. She was looking for quality not quantity. All he would be bringing was rubbish to the party. There would be no clowns allowed in her circle. It would be a circle of money, not a circle in a circus where there were less clowns than the men on this plane. She had checked them all out when they looked at her as she walked into the first-class seats.

She could see all their backstabbing eyes focused on her taking, a sneaky peek whilst their wives weren't looking. Little did they know most women have 300-degree vision against the tunnel vision men are usually born with. The only blind spot is the middle rear of the back of the head. Virtually every man on the plane wanted this woman to be theirs, candy on the arm and a bombshell in the bedroom, but they were all aware of the consequences of straying from the nest. It would cost more than half their fortune to move just a few seats away; straying would be futile to their bank account and businesses.

All she knew was that the lure had been cast, and it would only be a short time before she was reeling them in. There was no escape. The men were spellbound; her figure and beauty had captured them all.

CHAPTER 6

She moved into the hostess area where the food was stored, drinking Orangina like a praying mantis waiting to pounce on some gullible fool to come along and make conversation. She was on a mission to attract up to three men before the flight ended and get their phone numbers and addresses.

They were on their way into a Venus fly trap flower; the flower was fully open for business. All they had to do was fly in for the nectar, and the flower would close, and they would be devoured. She was the flower, and they were all being tricked to come and see. The funds would soon be coming in, and the diva would be on her way. No man out there would be winning the gold prize here; it was more likely to cost them gold to keep her in the lifestyle she was going to become accustomed to in the near future.

"More Orangina, Madam Sazzar?" the steward asked her.

"Yes, just a tad. Fill it to the top. I like a drink whilst I'm negotiating, sorry, chatting," she said clearing her throat of the Orangina she nearly choked on. This woman was dangerous to any man's wallet; money was money, she wasn't bothered. Fat or thin, small or tall, as long as they had substance she could relieve them of and make hers. Her preference was the short guys that talked a lot and shouted the loudest. It was easy for her to show them the right attention, and they were ready to buy her the world if it was for sale.

They are usually up there fighting for financial air to breathe, but they are the tigers of industry fighting above the rest. Perfect prey for a diva. She had one on the hook who was telling her how he made his fortune and how rich he was. *Yes,* she thought, *this one is in for the high jump, but he will never clear the bar where I'm going to set it. It's going to cost him a fortune for me to lower it for his height.*

He would have to fight for his top place at the diva's table. He had already said too much and spilled out his wealth to her, she was going to go to work on him. When she left, he would definitely know he was taken to the cleaners from the best. *I just love short men,* she whispered to herself. They were coming in droves to see her. As one left another took his place.

They were all fair game, she had what they wanted and were willing to pay the price. She was ready to accommodate them and take their money. It would be a match where everyone is a winner. They get to have her on their arm for dinner, she gets paid for looking glamorous and paying them the attention they were seeking. She knew exactly what they were seeking, but she was not going to go out there and sell herself cheap.

There was no price structure. If they wanted her company for a dinner dance, party, or function, they would have to pay the going rate for that day, depending on how rich they were. The only thing she would guarantee was service at its best. She wasn't an escort girl or pay-as-you-go; this lady was class, and if you wanted class, you had to dig deep in your pockets to afford a night out with the diva.

She was aware the competition was fierce out there, but nothing was in her league. She was out there a fledgling but had full knowledge about how to make money from men. All she had to do was point the way for them to follow. She was now in her element; she was in first class flying to the honeypot of Italy. There were going to be some rich people waiting for her there. All she needed to do was reel them in and strip them of their money and assets.

Her morals were those of a locust: go in the field and strip it bare. There would be no mercy shown or given; she was out to make money fast. Although she had some strategies to bring to the table, she was not short of charm and affection. This would all be an act, but if it was what her beneficiary required, she would meet his needs. The short guy had left the area and given her his card; he was like a lottery win to her.

She was exasperated by the number of men she had attracted to the rear of first class. She was a magnet, and they were all drawn to her -- she was dressed to kill. They were easy prey; she had them virtually eating out of her hand. She had four business cards and three phone numbers by the time she landed. She just had enough time to put a few small bottles of champagne in her large Louis Vuitton bag. She wasn't leaving first class without some benefit of paying all that money. *Well, okay,* she said to herself *I paid nothing and I'm out of here now, so watch out Italy, I'm here.*

The diva had arrived. As she came off the plane, she went through a passport lane for first class passengers. The man looked at her from behind the passport priority station, and she winked and walked straight through. He never even asked to see her visa. She was in without any scrutiny of her passport or visa; it showed her that money talks.

She was already up there with all those rich people breezing through passport control. She was out there with the best; she was on a roll. Things would not be difficult to obtain; everything was out there. All she had to do was make it hers. She cleared the customs and found herself out in the street. She had arranged accommodation through her friend on Facebook, so all she had to do was find her way there.

She waited outside and one of the men off the plane had a limousine waiting. The driver came to open the door for him, and he saw her waiting.

"Can I drop you somewhere, Madam Sazzar?"

"Yes," she said. "My driver is late; he will have to be reported to the company."

"No need for that, Madam," he replied. "I have plenty of room in here. Come and join me."

"Oh, thank you," the diva said. "That's so kind of you. Can you drop me at Melia Milano?"

"That a hotel?" the man said.

"Yes," she said, "it is."

"Well, it's not for someone as astute as you, Madam."

"Yes, I know. It was a late booking by my manager. She seems to get it wrong. I asked her to find the best place she could and that's all that was available."

"Not to worry, why don't you come to my house? I'm on the Amalfi coast not too far away. I have plenty of room."

"Well, it's an inconvenience. I would like to accept your offer, but I'm reluctant as I don't really know you."

"Don't worry about that. You're safe here with me, Madam. You will be looked after. Stay as long as you want. My butler will see to all your needs."

"Well," she said reluctantly, "I was going to find somewhere else, but I accept your kind gesture of accommodation. Its very kind of you to open your house to a stranger."

"Think nothing of it," the man replied. "My name is Gino; I know your name, Madam Sazzar. It's a lovely name. Your mother must have been a beautiful woman to bring someone like you up. It must have been a pleasure to have such a beautiful daughter."

"Yes, thank you," she replied. "My mother spent years thinking about a name to suit my lifestyle. We lived on the island in Lagos. We were middle class -- well slightly above," she said, putting her long legs into the back of the limo and sighing.

She had his eyes all over her, but she was a diva. She knew how to get someone's attention with that figure hugging dress, the long slender legs showing through the slit in the back. Just showing him enough to raise his blood pressure to over 200. He would need blood pressure tablets if he looked again. She was a temptress; it was all a game to her. Men were just a commodity she would buy and sell every day.

At the moment, she need somewhere to live and a large amount of spending money with someone to run her around in the limousine. She was on the first step of a long stairway; the learning curve was now reality and everything was happening now.

CHAPTER 7

A few hours ago, she had been boarding the plane to Italy from Nigeria. Now she was in a limousine with a rich good-looking guy whose eyes were undressing her as she fidgeted about on the seat, drawing him in even more. He was virtually frothing at the mouth; he was going to be easy bait for a diva. He would be cocooned in a spider's web; he just had no idea yet that it was coming.

She said, "it's so nice to be your friend. I can't wait to get to know you properly."

He was drinking out a bottle of water and he replied first before he swallowed, so it went all down his shirt. She giggled a bit as the embarrassed man laughed and said, "I think I was over eager there."

"Only a little bit," she replied. "Probably introductions are a bit nerve racking when you just meet someone," she said, lying through her teeth.

"Yes," he replied, "I do feel that way." She was as cool as a cucumber, she had him in the palm of her hands already.

He wanted something from her, and she knew it, but whatever he wanted was going to cost big money. He looked like he was wealthy, but she never took anybody on looks. She wanted them to show her the money. She was only interested in hard cash, no credit cards, definitely no Amex or credit facilities, all the cash up front. This lady would be marching him to the bank. If he wanted a credit facility, there was none.

It was a strange drive back to the house. Looking in his eyes there were dollar signs. He was looking at hers, she was showing love hearts to draw him in. She was not going to be caught in this love thing that wouldn't pay the bills, although it was a good tool to extract the dollars. She looked into his deep dark eyes. They were watering slightly; *he was in love*, she thought to herself.

I'm prepared to take euros. It's all the same to me. It's a good job they didn't still have the lira. No way would I have taken that; her thinking was of the scale to his. Je was mesmerised by her, and she was by his money. He wouldn't be a forever man, only if she wanted to keep him as a friend. If she was going through a dry spot, she would call him. For now, she was his property to play with, to take out on his arm and for fine dining. She would make him look like the man and take his status to another level.

So, she thought to herself *this is what I'm bringing to the party.* She just needed to know what he would be bringing. She was hoping for a good man with a big wallet and a passion to spend it on her. She would pay him all the attention he needed, but would he pay the price to go to a level of a girlfriend. She was open to marriage to the right person, this being a wealthy man.

She would accept no armchair dreamers; cash was king and that's what she wanted. She could be with the right man, but the only love she would have was the love of money. When you have grown up poor, you realise that money is right up there with health. You never want to do without it again; she was not going to fall in love with anyone that had holes in his trousers where the money had dropped out. Men with short arms and deep pockets were out.

She wanted the best and nothing else would do. She was on a roll now and she would be keeping this man happy for the near future. She would mingle with him and pick up on his friends' and their wives to be able to network herself into their lives. He would be a stepping stone into a lot of places, opening doors for her to be able to network her new friends. They would soon see her as the socialite, she was although real in her mind, the world of rich people was one of fantasy. There would always be rich people surrounded by the wannabes masquerading as rich aristocrats, movie producers, or wealthy businessmen.

She would have to make sure she did not ever attract dreamers, as they produce nothing but themselves. She had her man here, but what was he worth? Was he a captain of industry or an heir to a fortune, maybe a lottery winner? Although he didn't look like he had just won the lottery. They turned the corner and stopped in front of a large pair of gates with a security guard on the gate. The guard came to the car window and looked inside the car. He held a machine gun next to his chest, and he looked ready to use it. Another guard came out of the box with a machine gun and walked towards the car.

The guard looked again.

"Good afternoon, minister," he said.

"Good afternoon," the minister replied.

"Nice to have you back, sir."

"Yes, it's good to be home," he replied. The guard waved to the other one to open the gate. The car proceeded to drive down a long lane flanked with trees either side. The diva was starting to think to herself about her safety. *Who is this man was I'm sitting next to? Is he a boss of the mafia? Why the armed guards?* Her thoughts were running wild. Would she be stuck here with a mafia boss? Scared to go out for fear of being killed or kidnapped, she had made a big mistake getting in the limousine.

How on earth would she be able to get away? The car had driven around half a mile when she could see the road opening out, going to the left, and right in front of her the biggest house she had ever seen. This was an old building but beautiful in its design and quality. This was what she had been looking for all her life. She wanted to live in a mansion like this. It was magnificent; it looked bigger than the pictures she had seen of the Vatican and St Peters together.

Her mind had changed to one of a duchess, and her thoughts were running wild. She had won the jackpot. As long as he was clear of being involved in drugs, she was happy, she thought to herself. Walking around the house, giving her orders to the staff, she would be playing the role of the mistress of the house. They got to the door and the driver opened the door. It cut off the dream as he startled her. She had been in another dimension where she was floating around the house, gliding over the polished floor in a ball gown.

"Excuse me, madam," he said as he opened the door for her.

"Oh, yes, of course, sorry," she said as she got out of the car. She had been dreaming. Two men came out of the building dressed in suits and greeted them both.

"Good to see you back, sir, did you have a good trip?"

"Excellent" he replied as they opened the house door, "is everything okay with the dogs? They haven't been playing up?"

He said, "no, sir, they have been as good as gold, as usual."

"That's good. Meet my guest, Madam Sazzar."

"Pleased to meet you, madam," the man said.

"And you too," she replied.

"This way, madam," the man said, holding the door open, "would you like dinner at the usual time, sir?"

"Yes, I would think so. I will get settled in with the lady and let you know a time," Gino said.

"Thank you, sir," the man replied. "This way, madam, I will show you to your room. Is the one overlooking the garden at the rear suitable?"

"Yes, I'm sure our guest will be happy there. Can you see she has a drink and a snack before dinner, please?" Gino said to the butler.

"Yes, sir, I will instruct the kitchen to sort out the food," he said.

CHAPTER 8

"We haven't been formally introduced. My name is Gino. I could not tell you until I knew who you are and what your motives are for being in Italy. I am probably the biggest shareholder in most of the fashion houses in Italy, and I also own some of the top fashion brands around the world. We have to be careful, as spies come to pinch our fashion clothes to reproduce them in China. Italy is my place of birth, and this is where I make my living, but security is necessary as myself and my business have to be protected from kidnapping and ransoming. I am also the defence minister for the country.

"We live in a world where you have to protect yourself. I have never been a target, but it is for my own safety that I have the guards. My interests in you were not one of a girlfriend, but I see something in you that makes you stand out in a crowd. You know exactly how to make the right clothes look good and we were looking for somebody like yourself to be our next face of fashion in our fashion outlets. But it's not just that easy. There will be a lot of connections to make.

"I will personally take control of your presence in our empire of fashion; my staff will train you in all aspects of the modelling industry. It will be a one-time only offer. If you refuse, it will not be available again if you change your mind. So, I ask you now, as I am taking a risk on you as to whether you will be suitable for this position, but my instincts tell me I have found a jewel in the crown in you and I want to take you to the highest level. You will, of course, be my escort, and I will ensure your accommodation and flights are the best. You will accompany me to places around Europe and the world.

"I'm a married man so your wellbeing is safe with me. I would expect you to be an asset. You must have the company's best interests before your own, there will be no second chances. You will have to totally focus on your work, which would mainly be photography. I want you to be the face of 2025. You will be seen everywhere, on every fashion house brand, on every billboard, and in every magazine."

"You will be famous, but you have to commit yourself to me to take on the position I'm offering you."

Madam Sazzar was astonished by what he was offering. He wasn't a drug dealer or mafia boss. This man was the business king of Italy and possibly the world of fashion – also, he was a government minister. It seemed he was a man for whom anything he didn't own he didn't want. All the rest was his to control. He was, as we say in Nigeria, "The Man." He was a serious person that did not talk a lot, but she liked the fact he respected her for who she am.

She was a young lady from Nigeria trying to climb am impossible ladder, but she had struck gold with this man. He was decent and so good looking she was falling for him as she looked at this six-foot man with his dark hair and brown mysterious eyes. He was a dream man for her, with his olive skin and excellent posture; he was all a woman would ever want to see in the morning when she woke up. The downside was he smoked, and this she could not tolerate; she would have to get herself into a good status and try to get him to give up the smoking. It was not a habit she could live with, but his health would be a factor. If he gave up the cigarettes for good, it would be so nice to smell him as the man he was and not his cigarettes.

This man was not only a dream but a money magnet. What she really wanted to know was where his family was and if they lived in the mansion here. He had made no reference to them at all. Her vision was of his wife -- what kind of woman catches a man like this? He had everything a woman could want; he was perfect in every way. Impeccable in his dress sense, he had the best clothes she had ever seen. The quality was second to none, you felt his presence as he came into the room. He was everything she had dreamed about, but she was going beyond her remit. She was falling in love with a man she had only just met three hours ago on the plane.

She had been whisked away by him in his limousine; this was not the way she had seen her life going, but she needed what he was offering at this time. If she could get her picture everywhere, she would already be a famous face for the fashion brands, and she would be the woman to invite to all the parties, weddings, and functions of any type.

She would make an entrance into where the money was. After all that's what she did; she was going to be a diva. She now had herself on the ladder to success and she was going to milk every moment she was on top. She saw it as a slight diversion; it would not be a permanent situation, just a temporary one. No matter how rich and good looking he was, even Gino was fair game for this lady.

She showed no mercy; everything was about her, and she would not be taking any prisoners. There was a big wage cheque on its way, and, until it landed, she would keep her head down and go with the flow. There was no need to upset the equilibrium; she wanted a smooth ride into it all.

She would do the photos and commit six months at a long stop in the fashion industry, but she didn't want to work like everyone else. She was a socialite, a diva. Her career was never going to die out; she would be there still when she was old. The only difference would be that the numbers had changed: she was a diva, a socialite, but she would be having that title of diva and she would take it to the grave.

For now, she needed substance and that was money to spend, so she accepted the offer of being the face of fashion. She was ready for what was coming. She was going to create a suitable bank account for the monthly transfers. She was not going to be paying for anything; it would be on the house. She was going to have a minimum of six months and would hopefully be the face of fashion at the end. This would be a perfect exit strategy; she would be mixing in the right circles with the models and the dignitaries that came with the fashion industry.

She was going to make as many contacts as she could and would not leave until her book was full.

"Can I show you to your room, madam?" a maid said.

"Oh, yes please. I need to have a shower and clean up. You know what travelling is like, it leaves you wanting to clean yourself of the day's grime."

"Come this way," the maid said, "you can call me anytime day or night if you want anything, madam."

"Thank you," the diva said. "I will take your number down, and I will call if I need you, thank you very much."

CHAPTER 9

Gino was talking to the security men, and she thought he was instructing them to look after her welfare as he kept pointing her out. *Hopefully,* she thought, *precious cargo, that's going to cost a fortune.* But Gino was a very rich man, a billionaire -- money was nothing. He had it all. He was an empire builder and was a king of his fortune but, as we know, empires fall in time.

He was living his life as he saw fit. He would not be taking any stress; he was up there, the man of the moment. He had seen an opportunity and taken it. In his words, he was self-made. I was shown up to the room by the maid. The stairs to the mansion were amazing with the way they turned in different directions to access different parts of the upper floor space. The chandeliers above lit up the area, the light bouncing back off the marble floor.

This place was built for a king; she had never seen anything like it before. The maid opened the door, revealing a large double-windowed room. It was enormous. It had a four-poster bed in the middle of the room; it was exquisitely furnished. It was a different world to what she was used to. It was on a level she could have never dreamed about; it was something else. She even had her own computer station to be able to do her accounting on. It would be for adding up her wages and expenses she might incur, but the real use would be to call her friends around the world. After all, a diva had to have the tools to do her job.

It was a blessing, as she had never had the money to own a laptop, but it was top of the list to get the best laptop out there. If she hadn't got the best, she didn't want it. She would manage with the phone and desktop computer for the short term until she got what she wanted. She was on a roll, six months in modelling, and then she would have the face of fashion, and she could exploit her looks and figure into fame and fortune.

She would leave everything to happen. What was going to happen now would be fate, as she believed in fate, and she felt it followed her wherever she went. The diva would not be overstaying the mark; she had a plan and the next six months there were not a part of it. She had not foreseen the opportunity that she had been given, but she would not miss the chance of a lifetime to propel herself up a few steps of the ladder and get her closer to her goal of being a diva, a socialite with style and class.

She was ready for dinner. Everything would be happening there, Gino would be telling Madam Sazzar the plan he had and when it was all going to happen. She didn't want to be imprisoned in this mansion, no matter how beautiful. She had wings, and she was going to fly. The world was her oyster, and she wanted to be instrumental in the work she found and cash in on it.

She would be nobody's puppet, and her destiny was hers to control. Self-employment was what she was specifically engaged in and working for someone on a long-term basis was not in her remit. She was a rolling stone and wanted to make sure she went with the flow. No moss would be growing on this rolling stone.

She was clean, she didn't smoke, take drugs, or drink alcohol. There would be no vices to hold her back, and she would not surround herself with people that excessed in any of the bad vices as she would be cursed with it. Her only vice was money; she wanted as much as she could muster. There would be no holds barred in the way she would obtain it. Her money was hers for a rainy day.

She wouldn't spend a dime on anybody but herself. Her wealth would be paramount.

This, young lady, she thought to herself as she looked in the mirror. *I'm going places, baby; you're on the top of the world.* The maid knocked and she answered.

"Dinner, madam, is served."

She walked down the stairs; she looked like she had come out of a film with a long pencil thin dress on that she had rescued from the bin in Lagos. Though it was off a larger woman in a black silk type material, she had made some adjustments to make it fit her. She threw more away than she used, as it was an outsized dress, but she had made it fit like it had been shrunk onto her body. It showed every beautiful curve she had.

She was body-perfect for the dress she had made. As she walked down the stairs the butler met her.

"Madam," he said, "you are stunning."

"Thank you," the diva replied, "do you like my dress?"

"Madam, to like it would be an understatement. It's fabulous, is it?"

She stopped him. "No," she replied. "It's my own fashion."

Gino was sitting outside the dining room; he got up and took her into the room and said, "can you give me the designer of your dress? I would like to talk to him."

"You can talk to her now, if you like," she replied.

"Bellissimo, the dress is exquisite, and you designed and made this dress?"

"Yes, all with my own hand."

He said, "you're not only a beautiful woman, you are magnifico in your designs and taste. I would love to let you have a free hand in doing some outfits for our top ranges. I can see you are a multi-talented woman; your future will be one of a kind. You will have no competition here; you are the competition. Everybody will have to look over their shoulders to see you coming.

"I'm really looking forward to working with you, Madam Sazzar. It will be my pleasure to escort you to the table for dinner."

"Thank you," the diva replied, "for everything you have done for me."

"Well, don't thank me yet. You have a long way to go, and it will not be a walk in the park. It will be long hours, sometimes with little breaks, but the rewards for your work will be worth it all. Your status will go from an unknown to the face of fashion all over the world.

You will be one of the most photographed women in the universe.

"So, let's go into the dining room and have dinner and talk about money and what your schedule is for starting and transportation for us both, where you will be going."

They went into the dining room. The butler pulled back the seats to allow them access to the table.

"Madam," he said, "your seat is here."

"Thank you," she said as he accompanied her to the chair.

"And you, sir." He sat across from her. The table was too long to be able to talk comfortably without raising her voice. The nasty voice would only be for imbeciles that did not do their job properly as she had asked for.

Now it would be about her personality and impressing Gino enough, that it was not her persona. She had a brain besides her beautiful body, thanks to her mother and father who she blessed every day for her gift.

CHAPTER 10

She looked at the table. There were three forks of different sizes, three knives of different sizes, and three spoons again of different sizes. Where would she start? A panic set in. She had been lucky in Nigeria to get a fork or spoon. They were limited to what they had found thrown out by the middle class and salvaged by a young diva.

She was struggling to think what meals you ate with what cutlery. Then she remembered a film she had watched time and time again where, in the film, he showed the woman that you eat the first course from the knife and fork on the outside and work your way in to the last main course at the plate. It was the same with the spoons. She was hungry and ready for the first course; she had picked the right knife and fork up slightly off the table.

Gino looked over in amazement. "Well, dear I can see you have been bought up right. You wouldn't believe how many people pick up the wrong ones."

Wow, she thought in her head. *I'm glad I remembered the film. Otherwise I would have been typecast like the rest of them. I had class and it was shining through.* Gino could see it, and he smiled as she put the cutlery down. The diva had felt his presence in the room, but that had now dissolved into a more relaxed person. He was no longer the boss but a partner working with a beautiful, clever woman. Her heritage was not one of a poor person but as a diva that had come from good stock and would be more of a friend than an employee. A good travel companion. He was more relaxed like they had known each other for years.

She would not betray this man, although she was a diva, she could not betray him. She had taken him in as her friend, and she never would betray a friendship, although she had the morals of an alley cat. When it came to friendship, she was faithful to someone who would show the same respect.

They were served four courses; it was the most beautiful, tasty food she had ever tasted. They had a good conversation and her contract would be drawn up within the next week. Tomorrow they would go around the fashion houses in Italy and meet the staff and management, and they would meet the face and body of

Madam Sazzar. It was going to be interesting, but she could hold her own with anyone that would like to try it on with her.

She would never accept rubbish from anybody, not even the boss, but they were friends now and everything was as genuine as it could be. She was cruising and would be revealed to the fashion houses in the morning. They had a glass of champagne each and a brief chat and called it a night. I would be going to my room as the face of fashion. Who would have believed that a girl from Nigeria was now the face of fashion overnight worldwide?

It was a fairy tale come true. There would be no dreams tonight; she was now living the dream. The world was opening its door for her, her faith had seen her through, and she was now moving forward into another level. She was going to use what she had to make her way in life and to use what life had given her. She was young, she was attractive, and she would use what she had to go as far as she could. There would be no holds barred; she would max it out.

She was looking for contacts to add to her diary. Everyone she had would be an invite to an art collection, a party, a wedding, or a christening. She would make sure she was mixing in all the right circles; she had a mentor now in Gino. He would now be introducing her to all the people who worked for him or who were affiliated in some way. These were the people she would start with; she needed to mingle, and she was going to.

She would have filled two diaries by the time she was finished; her taste buds were dancing all over her tongue after the meal. She could have eaten it all again. How the other people lived! She want to become one of the other people and eat good food. The aeroplane food was better than what she had tasted in Nigeria as she was growing up. She was now grown up, but she had lacked food with proper nutrition: it was mainly white rice and whatever they could find to put with it. The odd plantain would be available but was not enough to sustain a healthy life.

The food now was going to give her the energy she needed to keep fit and healthy. There would be no more rice for her. She had seen enough bowls of rice to last a lifetime. She would never go back to those days; Gino was going to show her the good life. *The fast lane,* she called it, and she would be living in it. What would the employees think when she went into these blue-chip companies as a total unknown, and they were informed that she would be the new face of fashion? Eyebrows would be raised.

She would be moving up to the top of the ladder with the direct help of her mentor, Gino. He seemed a really kind man. How did this man get to be like a god within a lifetime? It seemed that it would take ten lifetimes to become the person he was. Did it come from his father or grandfather? She needed to know so she could understand where his wealth was generated from and learn from it.

She thought, *it could be me one day. Maybe, after the six months modelling, I could sidestep and look into more of a business in designing and retail and create my own brand.* Things were popping up in her head as she drank red wine, gazing out the large lounge windows. Thinking if she would ever be this lucky, she had her feet firmly on the ladder, and she was only going to be climbing. She would not be coming down without dynamite. That would be the only substance that would move her off my perch.

Gino had been attending to some business and walked into the lounge and sat across from her.

"We need to start your induction tomorrow, so we will be going to our biggest fashion house. There we will show you how it all works. We can get the designers to have a look around to see if they can find you some of our designer clothes and bags." Her eyes lit up when he said bags. She didn't have a designer bag -- she was not able to make bags as the material was scarce and they would have been difficult to sew.

She was going in with open eyes tomorrow. She had it in my head she might be able to obtain a designer bag at no cost. Nothing would be too good for this lady; she was cruising and ready to take on the world.

CHAPTER 11

A *free handbag would be nice* I thought. It was nothing to Gino to sort her one out. After all, I needed to look like the diva I was. I was going to be photographed everywhere, but I needed to focus on the work in hand. I couldn't afford to mess it up. I was going to be a top model for Gino's fashion house. I was sworn to secrecy on the brands I was the face for; he did not want anybody to know until the press release. I would have to tighten my lips to make sure I was not giving away too much.

Gino kept things very close to his chest, giving nothing away. He was here to put the right product in the right place at the right time. I was the product that would be seen all over the world. I was starting to get excited about the whole concept of being the face of fashion. This young girl from Nigeria was going to be known all over the world. It seemed that Gino had most of the top fashion houses in the world. What he didn't have or have shares in he didn't want.

There had to be some competition for him, although it seemed all his brands fought between themselves to be the pinnacle of his empire. I had the exclusivity of being his first choice, well, his only choice. He knew exactly what he was looking for and had seen it in me. I was so privileged to be in this position. He had elevated me to the top position above all the fashion models all over the world. I was his number one, and I was going to see to it that I would not let him down.

Everything was on hold until he had completed all the photography shoots and modelling of all the new brand of clothes. He had told me in confidence he had his eyes on the largest luxury brand for a takeover, he needed to be using the top models, and he was going to create the best in me. I was going to be the driver behind the new face of fashion and possibly instrumental in the takeover bid of the largest luxury brand.

He was going to put together a takeover bid and get them to call a shareholder meeting as Gino had a substantial shareholding in the luxury brand. This could be under his control based on the profits his company made on the turnover of the group of companies he owned. This would possibly sway the shareholders to vote in favour of a take over, as their share capital would go through the roof based on the new blood coming in from Gino and his ability to make large profits for the shareholders of the companies he owned outright or held shares in.

There would be no competition for him; *he* was the competition. He would put the diva out there mainly to unify the companies he owned to project the image of all the companies as one to dwarf the luxury brand he was looking to take over. He had his strategy, and I was part of it. Gino was a clever man, always thinking outside the box whilst keeping everything productive and creating avenues to take him to the next level. It seemed more wanted more, but this was what he did. He was a genius in the businesses. He was at the helm, and he would not be challenged in any takeover bids.

He was the man. Only he would be taking others over; I was now panicky that if it didn't go well, he would be ruthless in removing me from the position I was in and replacing me with someone else. I thought I was the ruthless one, but looking over at him drinking brandy next to the large fireplace against the roaring log fire, I could feel his brain working overtime. He was occasionally smiling when an idea in his head came together.

I think I was the best thing that had happened to him. It was my thinking that I needed him, but he probably needed me more, but I wouldn't dare put it to the test. Somehow, I don't think my feet would have touched the floor on the way out. I was too comfortable to rock the boat, so my best option was to smile and keep any thoughts to myself.

He was laughing about something, probably some deal he had struck at a good bargain price: he was always doing something. I had learned fast this man's brain never slept; he was always thinking. Business was his life, and it seemed that family was second, but his empire supported his family, and I could see a bit of myself in him. It might be the way I would be. After all he was giving his family a good life and standard of living but losing what the Italian culture was all about, family. Family life always came first, everything else was second, but Gino was a genius and had to do his work whilst he was young as everything about an empire like his would be difficult in later years.

CHAPTER 12

My focus was only on myself; what could this man do for me? We still had to settle on what payment I would be receiving for my services. Any money at this moment in time would be better than the 100 dollar note I had to my name, and I owed the taxi driver 25 dollars. He was never going to see it; I wouldn't be back there ever. My life was now here in the luxury of Gino's empire in Europe and the westernised countries around the world.

We were ready to travel in the morning; he was taking me to the head office in Milan. He said if we had time he would show me the sights of Milan. It had been a dream of mine to see where the Romans had existed in older times. I was now hoping it would be a whirlwind tour of the offices. I wondered why he was taking me to the office in place of the factories where the clothes were made.

My best guess was that most of the fashion clothing stock was made abroad. It would be interesting to know more about the business and how it all worked. We said our good nights to each other and went to our rooms. He was obviously staying and not going home to his family. They probably lived a fair distance away, in Rome, possibly.

I would have to ask him, but I had found out in life there is a right time and a wrong time to ask personal questions. This was not the time to become too personal about his private life; my focus should just be on the fast progression of my career. The diva was on hold until I had become the face of fashion.

I had a long shower. It was so invigorating. I had never had the luxury of wasting water; before it was a bucket hung outside with holes in it and filled up with water, sometimes the water was dirtier than we were but we all showered once a week if we were lucky. I was here now, having the time of my life, and I didn't want it to stop.

I got into bed; it was still light outside, but I wanted to feel the luxury of sleeping in a four-poster bed where if you turned in the night you wouldn't fall out of the bed. I lay there with the feather pillows under my neck. It was like being in heaven; it was bliss. We were lucky to have a pillow at home, they were filled with straw and coconut husks, not really a good night's sleep on one of those.

This was five-star luxury, there could not be anything better. The house was truly magnificent; I lay there half expecting a knock on the door from Gino wanting a chat or something more. I wasn't sure about the something more. I was still a virgin, and I was not going to give it away to any man for money alone. There would have to be love and a promise of forever. My man would have to be gentle and kind and a stallion at the same time in the bedroom.

How could I know whether I had chosen the right man when we had never been intermitted? It would be a lucky dip. Maybe I would have to just go for the money at first and forget the virginity. At least I would know what I would be getting in the bedroom. I was looking for a thoroughbred racehorse, not a donkey. It was against all my morals to make out with a man before being married, but the rules had changed. I needed to know I had the right man before committing to anyone. It would be a preselection process.

I would have to learn about the man before entering his bedroom; I was not that type of girl. Money was my main objective. It would never let me down like a man would sometimes. I had witnessed it at home in Africa: the boys only wanted me for one thing, and it wasn't my intellect, it was always something more personal I was still attached too. It was going to be time to enjoy myself but focus mainly on my modelling and being in the right places and with the right people to become a socialite and eventually a diva.

I must have fallen asleep; it was morning I heard a knock on the door. I put on my free dressing gown out of the bathroom and ran to open the bedroom door with not a stitch on but the gown. As I opened the door, the belt I had around it was not fastened, and it fell off. The gown opened up. There I stood as the door opened, showing everything.

"Hello madam," the man said. "Sorry, but I'm taking over today from Manwell. Would you like some breakfast, madam?"

I breathed a sigh of relief. "Thank god," I said in a split second, grabbing the belt of the gown and fastening it up.

"Yes, I would love some, please," I said. Madam Sazzar was fully composed and ready for breakfast.

Thank the lord it was not Manwell or, even worse, Gino; I would have had a hard time convincing him it was just the fact I had not fastened the belt properly and it fell off, revealing my birthday suit. He was a man with morals, and he took his business very seriously. A break from the matrimonial house to my bedroom would not have been a good call.

I had to stop thinking that something might happen. I had to think differently, but the man was handsome, older but well-mannered and on top of that a billionaire or close to it. I was coming down to ground level. I asked myself what this man would want with a woman probably less than thirty years younger. Although I was mature in body and mind, I had never looked at an older man before, but all options were open now to discover my preferences and how I would see my first real love: with a mature man who would teach me everything or a younger man with whom we could spend time being young and in love but with no experience of life.

What was I saying to myself was, why the hell would I want to keep jumping over hurdles all the time? I had finished my learning curve. Yes, I was still a virgin, but I now knew what I was looking for and there was a big ocean full of fish. I was the fish they wanted. I was not going to be an easy fish to reel in, I would be fighting like a marlin and those not capable of landing the catch would be stabbed with the sword.

I was an open-ocean, fast-living fish, and I needed a man that would be able to keep up with me everywhere, including the bedroom. I didn't want to see him in the bedroom defeated and out of breath. I needed a man with stamina to feed my lust for love. I would be setting out all the parameters to guide him and the hurdles to jump over. He was going to have to be everything all rolled into one.

I was free of the ties of Africa, and I was blazing a trail that only the best could follow.

CHAPTER 13

Her man would have to be tall, dark, and handsome with integrity and to know her as the woman she was. She would not be controlled by any man, so he would have to understand his position in their relationship. She was nobody's fool and never was going to start to be one. She was so far ahead of anybody that thought she would be a woman that was thinking or if he couldn't support her he wouldn't last the night. Her thinking was, if he is bringing nothing to the party, he wouldn't be invited.

The perfect man was out there somewhere but finding him was not a priority. She had other things to think about besides a man; she was fully focused on the trip tomorrow to the offices and workshops in Milan. She was looking to grab a nice bag if one was available. She had never owned a nice bag; in fact, she had never owned anything nice. Nice was a luxury she couldn't afford; she was looking to go up market to something that would be a statement as she walked into a room.

She wanted a nice skirt and matching jacket to make her look important as they travelled around the world. Gino was introducing her as the face of fashion -- she was on a roll, *pinch me,* she thought, *this could not be true. I'm going to be famous; I've been here less than a day.* She hoped he was going to keep his word and do what he said he would. She would be devastated if he or somebody changed his mind, after all could a lady from Nigeria pull this off.

Her family would all need smelling salts to bring them around when they saw her in world magazines. She was going to phone her siblings and parents as soon as she started the photo shoots. They would not believe that she could be so successful in such a short time and would have to read it to believe it. The more she thought about it, the more excited she was becoming.

They had breakfast fit for a king, although she needed to keep her model figure and it wouldn't go down well if she started putting on the pounds. She would have to resist the fine dining out or make sure she ate the main course only. She was not used to eating, never mind three course meals, it was never going to be something she could commit to as it was paramount to her that her figure stayed as it was.

She was tall, she was slim, she was sexy, and she was over here in Italy, one of the most fashionable places in the world. This was her oyster, and she was going to indulge in everything offered to her on a plate. This was her idea of heaven, and she had arrived.

Gino came into the dining room. "Are you ready to go, Madam Sazzar?" he said

"Yes, I'm ready," she replied.

"Okay, the helicopter is waiting outside."

"Helicopter?" she said. "Are we going in a helicopter?"

"Yes," Gino replied.

"Oh," she said. "I've never been in one before."

Gino said, "well, I was a bit apprehensive on my first helicopter ride, but its more or less a daily commute to the business premises. There is too much traffic to drive in."

"I'm so excited," she said to Gino.

"That's good, I like a lady that appreciates style."

"Yes," she said, "I definitely appreciate style."

She was thinking, *I waited all my life for this,* but her lips were sealed. She didn't want Gino to know her roots and where she had come from -- a really poor background.

Her thinking was that if he knew, he might not be too keen to take her on as the face of fashion.

He smiled and said, "let's go. We have a lot to do today."

They went out to the rear lawn. There it was. It was fabulous; it was a large silver and metallic blue helicopter. It looked stunning.

The pilot was starting the engine, and she could see the rotor blades starting to turn round, getting faster as they moved to the inside, up the steps. All the seats were white leather, it was luxurious. She had never seen anything like this, never mind been in one. There was writing on the outside of the helicopter which said, International Fashion Inc. When she asked him if this was the name of the company he said, "yes, it's one of them."

Wow, she thought, *just one of them.*

He said, "it's our New York fashion house. Our helicopter for here is on its way; it was a special order, so we are going to ship this one to the USA as the one we have over there is due for renewal. So, we are sending them this one." She was trying to put it all together. *So he has three helicopters. How many more does he have? This man is so rich it's unbelievable,* she thought to herself, her mind was running wild. How much money was his company worth? It seemed nothing was beyond his reach. What else did he own besides this? It was going to be an experience to find out.

She was intrigued by his lifestyle. She could not comprehend how much money this man had, he was richer than the whole of Nigeria, she thought. The helicopter started to take off and they were on our way; Gino was pointing out places of interest. It meant nothing to her as she had never been out of Nigeria, never mind Italy and all its splendour. She was happy she had chosen this as her first place; she would not be looking back now. Everything was ahead of her now.

"How far is it now to the factory?"

"Oh, not far now, we should be there in eight minutes," he replied. She sat there fidgeting about trying to see different views from each side of the helicopter.

CHAPTER 14

"Here it is," he said.

She looked down and said, "what are all those buildings down there?"

He said, "that's our factory."

"What?" she said. "All those buildings?"

"Yes," he said.

"But it's so big."

He said, "yes, love, it is where we turn out a lot of clothes and bags from there."

"I'm very impressed," she replied. "It's like a city down there."

"Yes," he said. "We have added a lot to it over the years as we increased the fashion brands we sell. You have heard about our fashion brands?"

"Heard about them, of course. They're famous around the world."

"Yes, I suppose they are," he said. "I don't get too involved with world sales. I tend to spend my time around here and in the USA.

"I'm just looking at the figures and how the sales are performing between the companies. I like to know what's happening in the world markets of fashion, who is making all the leaps and bounds in the current markets. We need to be at the top, always, to stay competitive in the global marketplace."

"Yes, of course, I have heard so much about your fashion brands and actually read your autobiography. I never knew it was you and that I would meet such a fashion magnet. I did not make the connection between you and the fashion brands you own.

"It's amazing to be in your company, I just loved your book. I was intrigued by your story; you came from a working-class background like me and here you are now, a fashion mogul."

"Well, I wouldn't put it like that," Gino replied, "but you're not too far away with your description of me, although I would like to think I was a businessman with benefits." *Benefits*, the diva thought, *I would say so: helicopters, private jets, first class travel, mansions to live in, waiting on staff, security staff, gardeners, maintenance staff. He was an empire builder, and I was already in love with him.*

His mind was on another level to anybody else that she had ever known. She needed to learn from this man. Gino was a captain of industry and retail yet selective in his fashion brands, he didn't want to own it all, only the best fashion houses. He was here for quality not quantity, only the best would do. He dressed the best he had style; it was easy for him. He never had to make his own clothes like she did; he had them made exclusively for him.

The difference in quality would be on a different scale, but the designs could have been world-beating with the correct fashion house to push her designs. Maybe she might be able to help design clothes as well, that might be the next step after the face of fashion. *Next step?* she thought to herself. *Where was my thinking going? it sounded too much like work. I'm not going there,* she thought to herself.

I've not come all this way to end off in an office designing clothes. I want to make sure I'm living the life not working all my life. Work was not on the radar for her, a bit of face modelling surely couldn't be that hard to do, after all Gino would be looking after her. What a man to be her mentor. The offices were fabulous, all marble walls and floors, shining glass partitions throughout. The lighting seemed to bounce off the floors to the walls like it was dancing. The light coming through the windows was magnificent, the way it had been channelled through in beams bursting with energy, keeping everything in a show of light. As the clouds moved across the sun, it looked like it had been a design feature for a 21st century dreamhouse.

It was amazing to be a guest there. It would have been a fabulous place to work in, but that word work was no longer going to be in her vocabulary. It had to be erased from her mind; it would not be a word she wanted to hear again unless it was for someone else and their experience at work. It would be incomprehensible for her to do anything that included working hard, but with the environment that Gino had created in the offices, people came to work seemed happy to be here. After all, the vitamin D that came through the windows every day from the sun was so good for their wellbeing.

Vitamin D was never in short supply in Nigeria; we overdosed on it. She was glad to be away from the 40-degree summers and winters. There was no comfortable heat to be in, it was always hot, but things were on the change. She was here in Milan, one of the world's fashion capitals, and she was going to be instrumental in changing the face of fashion for 24/25. She was already hoping to be the face of fashion for 25/26, getting a little above her station.

She was still floating around the fact she was going to be famous in every fashion shop, every magazine, TV shows… She was well on the way to take the crown for her year of fashion modelling. Where would she go from there? Would she possibly take her chance at modelling? Who knows where it would take her. After all, she had the king of fashion behind her; it could only be an upwards move. She was not about to do a downward spiral, that would be a definite no, no, that could never be her. She had been born a winner, losing was never an option. Onwards and upwards had always been a goal of hers, a dream to be the best, second was never in her remit.

It was introduction time. First of all, they were going to meet the office staff. They were all lined up in the meeting room, ready to meet them like celebrities. This was what she was born for, this was what her whole life was waiting for: these people were the hub of the office. Staff for all of Europe and everything went through these people here, all the orders and designs. There must have been over two hundred office staff, the place was enormous. She had to be introduced to all the staff, she was not sure what she would be doing there.

She thought Gino has set it all up as a surprise. She was a bit nervous – it was not like her, but all the people were intrigued to know what was happening and who was the African girl Gino was introducing into the business. What part would she be involved with? Thoughts were flashing through her head. Would they welcome her or would there be a vote of no confidence?

She was here to stay, and nobody would make her feel uncomfortable. She was Gino's choice, and she was excited now. He was about to do his speech. She was trembling inside but so happy on the outside. This was her moment to be accepted by all the office staff. Gino stood on a step and the room went quiet. He started speaking, and there was a bit of rustling from a few of the ladies standing together. They were pointing to her and discussing her and Gino. She thought they were trying to put them together as an item, which would not be true, although he was every girl's dream.

He was a married man, and she respected him as such. He had a beautiful family, and she was not going to be the reason to break it up. They were just being bitches trying to create a fire where there was no smoke.

CHAPTER 15

I would never be Gino's woman. He already had one, and I would not be instrumental to breaking up their marriage or even testing Gino to see if he would go for it. He was my friend, and I would not betray a confidence. Gino was such a nice man he was a true gentleman. He was a man you could keep as a friend forever; I didn't want to have the typical boss-employee relationship. I respected his choice that he put his family first.

I was happy to be a cog in this big wheel and generate as much capital and exposure for his products as I could. I would not be looking for any media exposure between me and Gino; I was totally focused on the job in hand. That was looking good and being the face of fashion. I couldn't stop referring to that statement. I was so in love with the story, Nigerian girl to the fashion capital of Italy and the fashion houses I would be representing on a daily basis.

We would have time to get to know each other, I was not sure how long it would take me to know Gino as the man he was. I would not want to take it beyond that level. We were best friends, and I was grateful for the respect he showed me. Gino was now on a platform where he could see all the staff. We had been down the line of staff and finished our introductions. He hadn't asked the names of the staff only introducing me as Madam Sazzar. There had been a few eyebrows lifted when he said my name. It was a lot to take in, but a woman has to get her attention somewhere.

My new name was a good start, I could see them grouping and talking about me, wondering what would this Nigerian woman have so much attention from the boss Gino for and why was he introducing her. She had them all thinking he had made a commitment and was about to follow through on a speech. I was really nervous now, virtually ready to run out of the room, but I owed it to myself and Gino to remain standing. Although I was desperate to sit down and disappear rather than face the crowd. What would they all be thinking?

They had met this young lady and was about to be introduced formally by Gino the managing director of the international fashion corporation. I was shaking going up the steps to join him, I would have rather gone without a meal for a week than go on that platform with him in front of all his staff.

"You're in good hands," Gino said as I stood beside him. He started his speech "to all my loyal staff old and new I would like to take this opportunity to introduce our new employee of International Fashion Corporation, Madam Sazzar.

"She will be our new face of fashion for 24/25. I would like everybody to welcome her into our family and give her our best wishes for this year ahead." There were a few murmurs in the crowd, some happy faces and some not so happy. Gino said, "please welcome her to our family," and he started clapping and everybody else joined in. It was a lovely greeting for me, and I relaxed from the nervous tension I had been feeling.

I could see that, for some of the staff, it was a shock to see this Nigerian lady standing next to the boss. Who was presenting her? What agency had to decide to make her the face of fashion? Where had she come from? Was she allowed to be here? Did she have the right? She was already in place and she looked a million dollars. Gino had already commented on how beautiful and stylish she looked in her skirt and coat all hand made by herself.

She had a talent to know how to look amazing, she was taking the fashion to the next level.

Her style was nowhere else, and everyone was pointing to her clothes. They were a style never imitated or copied by other designers. These were a new take on fashion, the styling was from another era in the future. In the style and the materials, she was already trendsetting and out-classing most of the latest designs. They had a warm welcome from the office staff, and they needed to go and meet the staff in the design studio and the models that catwalk the garments at the shows.

Gino employed everybody directly. There were no agencies in the life of a fashion magnet, a billionaire. He was the man of his era. There were no contenders for his crown. He had won through being proactive in his business. He was even picking his face of fashion now; I was hoping he had made the right choice. I didn't want to let him down; he had seen something in me I hadn't seen myself. To put me on a pedestal was such an honour, and I was beaming as we entered the designer warehouses.

He was going to keep it local as we had gone past lunch. We were getting hungry and needed to eat, but I was hyped up not over feeling lunch as I needed everybody to see what Gino had seen in me. I didn't want to look bloated. I needed to keep myself looking like a goddess. I was on a roll, and I was going for it, we were going for a tour around the factory, all the eyes were on me walking around with the big boss. I felt so important. That meeting outside the airport had paid dividends.

I was a celebrity already. Everybody commented on my jacket and skirt and were asking where I purchased it. I told them I designed and made it myself out of reclaimed fabric, and they were astounded at the talent I had. Everyone was so kind on the designer section, and we moved into the fitting rooms. There were groups of girls trying on clothes and doing a virtual catwalk in them.

These were Gino's models; they were all different shapes and sizes. This was not how the fashion industry worked, but he was now cat-walking clothes for the larger ladies. As well as the size 8s, he was doing up to size 18. His clothes were the height of fashion whatever the size. Fashion was taking a step away from the stereo type modelling and moving on to fit an emerging market covering most sizes of women and men. There was a large market for all sizes, and Gino wouldn't be left behind or stereotyped into one size fits all if you're a 6 or an 8.

I could see them looking over at me in their groups. Bad news always travels fast. They had got wind of me being the next face of fashion, and you could clearly see they were not happy with me as I was an outsider taking their jobs. They were full of poison, and I think I was in for a bite. Gino left to see the manager of the department we had met earlier in our introductions; he had left me unknowingly in a nest of vipers. They were not happy, but they had been asked to look after me whilst he was in the meeting.

I was okay. I could look after myself; I had experience of jealously before. I could see the way they were looking at me was not going to be a good experience. These women were not here to help me up but to trip me up. They didn't like me before I was introduced to them, they disliked me even more now they know who I am. There was a group next to us; I could hear them talking. As I was listening to my group, I heard them say "that bitch is to be the face of fashion, she will be plastered all over the magazines and walls. She is a tramp."

Well, I think *tramp* was the word that set me off the most, and I went over to the group and told the one that said it that if she let her loose lips go again, she would be the one plastered over the walls. Literally. This was a vicious place to work amongst all these women, but I could give as much as I took. I'd had to fight for food, so fighting for money and fame would be a walk in the park for someone like me. Nobody was going to be able to stab me in the back. The claws were out now, and trouble was on its way.

I had the title, and none of these vixens were going to take it away from me. I wouldn't be going anywhere. I was here for the long haul; I was going to see it out until the end, whenever it came. I was not going to be bullied out by a bunch of foxes; they would be taking on more than they could handle with me. I had fought for everything I had ever had, there was no easy life for me growing up.

CHAPTER 16

I had definitely marked their cards, and they now knew where the boundaries were. If they came into my space again, I would do exactly what I said. I would ensure that justice was served. There was no pussycat here -- underneath I was a lion and trouble would be theirs. When I came, there would be no holds barred, my mother had always told me that if you bring trouble to your own door, you have to live with it.

I was no one's fool, and they better not try and make me look like one. I had been with people like this before and I was not going to play their games. Gino had come back and was talking to the models. I looked over and they looked away. I think I had left my mark; I was the important one here now, not them. I was the person that would be taking the crown now, so I could walk out holding my head high. I hoped my words would go around fast, as I would not be getting involved in any trouble that might rear its head when I was the face of fashion.

All that fighting would be behind me; I would be one of the most photographed women in the world. I had come a long way in such a short time. I was now on my way up, and I was young enough to stay up if I watched my enemies, as they would like to see me fall. We had seen everything we needed to, and Gino had booked a table at a famous restaurant in Milan. He was taking me there now.

There was a helipad on the roof, so it would be only a short journey, around 10 minutes, and we would be there. Everything was the best with Gino, nothing was left to second best. His motto was that he hadn't worked this hard to be a nobody, and he was right; he was a giant in his business portfolio. He would have the best or go without, I had learned that from him. He said he hadn't come all this way not to be able to have the best.

We landed on the roof deck and staff came out to welcome us to the restaurant. It was very high up and the wind was blowing badly, but we had to leave and go inside. I was hungry, I'm not sure what for. Gino was the man, and most women are hungry for the man, but I had to keep focused on the job. *Gino is my boss,* I said to myself, and I made a promise to myself never to sleep with my boss. That would not end well and never did in work relationships, it was a no-go area for me. Although you can't help who you fall in love with; a person can be in love with another without even knowing.

I was up for work only and it would never be something I invited. My career was the most important thing to me, as was staying a virgin, although at times I felt ready to make love with the right man and it was a hard job to find him, wherever he was hiding. I would only accept the best; no dreamers were going to come into my life. I had left them behind me, and I knew they were all over the world. *Freeloaders* I used to call them; there would be no room in my life for any of them.

I was on my way up and no nonstarter was going to drag me down to where I was, living for the next meal. Poverty had left my thinking the way it is now; I was never going back. It was going to be hard work every day, but you only get out what you put in. I would make sure I stayed at the top. Going back was not an option. All my visas and right to work were all now in place. Gino had seen to it all; he was my knight in shining armour.

I would never lose him as a friend, tomorrow we were going to Paris. I was so excited. We were going to New York as well, when my visa arrived, but Paris was on my mind. He was going to show me some of the outlets that sell the products they produce, such as clothes, shoes, bags, and accessories. I was so ready for everything he showed me; I was relentless in pursuits of all the good things in life.

Gino had it all, and I was overzealous to learn about it all. I wanted to start work now, but I had to wait for everything to be in place. We had not even signed contracts yet with Gino, and I wasn't sure how much I would be getting paid. It was under negotiation. When I asked him, he waited to see how I was as a person to try and gauge whether to pay me the same as the face of fashion that was now at the end or to increase the salary for 24/25.

I think Gino had dangled a carrot for me to bite on. He just wanted to know just how much I wanted the job, but I understood all contracts had to be prepared and in order before I was employed on a contract basis. I was feeling impatient but was loving the attention and the trips out with Gino. He was the perfect host, tall, dark, handsome, and very rich -- what more could a girl ask for? He was the full package, and he was not only my boss, but also my friend.

I was so lucky to know him, and I said a prayer every day for him. We were going to Paris on Friday, which was three days away. Gino was having some time with his family and would not be back until Thursday night ready for Friday in Paris. We would be flying there; it was a long trip in a helicopter. Gino had sorted out tickets, first class, obviously -- there was nothing but the best for me now. I would soon be the diva I always wanted to be. Okay I would have to work for my fame, but it would all come soon.

I was ready to take on the challenge. I was ready to relax. Gino said he had a present for me, just a thank you for letting him show me around. Now I was intrigued as to what the present was, as I hadn't done a lot, but all presents would be appreciated no matter how small. We got in the helicopter back to the mansion house; the pilot remained in the helicopter waiting for Gino to come back.

He was at the airport to Rome tonight. It was nice, as he was a family man, and I liked that he spent time with them. It would be good here, chilling out, living like a princess in his palace. I was here as his guest, and I would enjoy the pleasures of his accommodation as had been awarded me. He said goodbye and was on his way. The butler asked me what time I was ready for dinner.

I said, "give me time to have a shower and change and I will be ready around 7pm."

"Okay, madam," the butler replied.

I must ask his name tonight I can't keep calling him the butler. The diva opened the door to her room. The light was streaming through the bedroom, dancing on the walls in a show of light. The four-poster bed, the main attraction, and the chaise lounges under the windows looked so different and inviting when the sun was out. I was in my heaven. Everything in here is what I had dreamed about as a young girl reading magazines. That one day was here, it had arrived with thanks to Gino. I had gone to heaven and was loving it.

CHAPTER 17

It would be hard to ever equal what he had worked for; it was magnificent, and here I was as his guest in his mansion. I hoped it would last forever, but my feet were firmly on the ground. I wanted a piece of the life Gino had made; he would be my mentor. I would never have his business brain, but my looks and fashion would hopefully carry me through to better times and a better lifestyle. This is where I wanted to be, at this level, before I was 40 years old. I would have to ensure I followed his lead in business, kept my eye on the ball, and did not take my eye off it until I owned it all.

I laid on the chaise lounge thinking about everything and looking out over the beautiful gardens. Everything was perfect here; I had been daydreaming and nearly fell asleep. I needed to shower and get ready. Just because Gino wasn't here did not mean I didn't have to make an effort to get dressed for dinner. I wanted to look my best for Gino so his staff could show him and me respect even in his absence.

He was probably in Rome by now. I wished him all the best. He deserved everything he had ever worked for and the risks he had taken to amass his empire. He was an amazing man. I was ready and the butler knocked on my door. I opened it to see him holding a parcel.

"By the way, madam," the butler said. "I have a delivery for you."

"Thank you," Madam Sazzar said. "I will be down shortly."

"Yes, madam," the butler said. "Would you like the menu, madam?"

"No, thank you," she said. "I'm sure I will find something on there I like."

"Okay, madam, is there anything else?" the butler said.

"Well, you can leave me the present."

"Oh, I'm so sorry, madam, your beauty took my mind away from me for a minute."

"That's alright," I said. "You're welcome."

"Thank you, madam," he replied. "I will see you soon."

"Yes, of course," I replied and took the parcel and shut the door.

I was intrigued as to what was in the parcel. Should she open it now or wait until later? I couldn't stop herself opening it. There it was: one of the most expensive handbags in the world and a card saying *with gratitude, Gino. Wow,* I thought. This was beautiful, the handbag and the card. I knew the brand well, it was even out of the reach of rich people. Gino had looked after me so well. Was there no end to his generosity? He was a good man but also a businessman. Would the bag be reflected in my salary? I was happy just to have it.

They had a three-year waiting list to get a bag like this, and the cost would make a rich man's eyes water. This was the top of the draw handbag; I had made the right impression on Gino, and he was rewarding me for my beauty and confidence. He was the best man I had ever known, excepting my parents. He had taken me under his wing, as they say, and he had turned out to be my mentor. Nothing he asked would be too much for me to do.

I had my bag for dinner, although there was nothing in it. I would represent myself and Gino amongst the staff. I might have a walk around the gardens later with my bag. I felt so special as I opened the door and made my way down the staircase to the dining room. I felt like a

queen as I came down the stairway. It was so beautiful --
fit for a queen, definitely. The butler was in the hallway
waiting for me as I arrived.

"Excuse me," Madam Sazzar said, "can you tell me
your name, please? I can't ignore it anymore."

"Yes, madam, its Marco."

"Oh good," she replied.

"That's a nice name," I said.

"Yes, madam, it was my late father's name."

"Do you mind if I call you Marco?"

"Not at all, madam," Marco replied.

"Well, I shall call you Marco in the future."

"Thank you, madam, but not too much in front of
the boss."

"Oh no," I said, "I don't want to get you into trouble."

"Thank you, madam. Your table is ready. Would you
like to be seated?"

"Yes, that would be nice. I'm hungry and ready for
my dinner." I was so hungry I ate it so fast like when I
was in Nigeria and we had to eat quickly or it was all
gone fast when we had food. I would have to eat only the
right food as I needed to maintain my figure.

I was going to be on show all the time and needed to
look good for the photos to show Gino he had made the

right choice. Choosing me was a good decision of his, he was a good judge of character as he spoke to me a lot before offering me the job. I couldn't wait for his return; we were going to Paris. I had never been anywhere but Milan which I would see whilst Gino was away if Marco could call me a taxi one day so I could go around one of the fashion capitals of the world.

I had read about it but never been out of Nigeria, so everything my eyes encompassed would be a first. I wanted to be out there, walking the streets, looking at the new fashion shops discovering what was out there. I had been shut away all my life. My only contact with the fashion world was reading old, discarded fashion magazines. I had never witnessed the reality of being here in Milan, where I could feast my eyes on the latest fashions.

I was excited to be going out. I would ask Marco to call me a taxi after breakfast. The morning couldn't come fast enough. I wanted so badly to feel free. Although I was in luxury, it would be a prison for three days. I needed to spread my wings a bit and get out into where life was bustling and the streets were full of people. I needed to see and be seen in the cafés and restaurants.

I would have to look good, as I was soon to be famous. The future was bright, and I was bathing in full sunshine. This was my time, and I was going to enjoy it to the max. There were no limits on the things I would be doing, my future was here, and there was no time like the present to enjoy my life.

Living in the fast lane, it was all out there for the taking, and I was instrumental in taking it all. Morning came fast; I was still asleep when Marco knocked on the door.

"I will be 15 minutes," I shouted at the door, I had projected my voice from the bed, one of my talents I had learned in Nigeria.

"Thank you, madam," Marco replied. I showered and was ready in 10 minutes -- my hair would have to wait until later. I was fully focused on having breakfast and getting the taxi into Milan.

As I walked down the stairs, Marco was waiting for me

"Good morning, madam," he said.

"Good morning, Marco," I replied. "I want to go into Milan after breakfast. Would you call me a taxi for around 10am?"

"Yes, of course, madam," he said. "You won't need a taxi; the guards will take you and wait for you outside the shops you want to visit. I'm afraid the boss left strict instructions that you were to be accompanied everywhere you want for your safety, madam."

CHAPTER 18

"What, for my safety?" I replied.

"Yes, madam. The word is out now that you are to be the face of fashion, and you have become a target for kidnappers or criminals. You need to be guarded when in the cities, as they are not safe for you to walk around without protection."

"I'm astounded by what you have said, Marco. How can this be? I have lived in Africa all my life."

"Well, madam, you weren't going to be the face of fashion then like you are now. You might have a price on your head with the local mafia, and it's not safe for you to wonder the streets on your own. Desperate people take desperate measures when it comes to money, and you would be a target for ransom. It may never happen, but the boss said you will need protection in the city. Whilst you're with him he feels you need to be protected as a precaution.

"You can go when you want to, but the guards will have to wait outside for you. He left you a credit card and pin number should you require something nice."

"I will be alright with my own money, thank you, Marco," I replied "I will do what Gino wants me to do. He knows best. I'm sure he has evaluated the risk factors, and I accept this decision and will stay close to the guards. Do they have guns?"

"Oh yes, they are licensed to have them for your protection and the boss's. They have never needed to use them, but the boss would be a high prize to potential kidnappers, so he is protected wherever he goes. It's for your protection."

"Well, I should see it as an honour that he sees me as a celebrity."

"Yes, madam," Marco replied. "You would be best to take his instructions on this, madam. You don't want to be going on your own -- it wouldn't be a wise move."

I took his advice. I did not want to disregard it, as this would put me in an awkward position with Gino, like I was some kind of maverick. I decided just to have a tour of the city, but I would stay in the limousine and just get out to window shop. I was not in the habit of putting myself in situations, as Africa was wild at night, and I was never out late there.

The guards bought the car to the entrance. I was ready to get in and go. I had limited money, but I didn't want to take up Gino's offer of a credit card. If I spent his money, he would think differently about me. I was better off using my own money and retaining my self-respect, totally the opposite to my thinking of paying for nothing, but I was now with the man. He was a global mogul, and I always wanted to remain on his good side. Sometimes you have to concede to succeed in life. Nobody wants somebody that wants to extract the goodness out of a person.

I would only expect what Gino wanted to give and never push the boundaries beyond my remit. We were happy working together and that's the way I wanted it to stay. We were friends, and I never betrayed a friendship. I would not be extending my welcome beyond today; it would be one day of sightseeing, and I would spend the rest of the time at the mansion until Gino arrived back.

We got into Milan; the city was lovely but spoiled by the graffiti in places, like lots of cities, but the shops were amazing. The way they were set out to sell clothes, they had it right; people shopping here were class. There were no dreamers here, people had money to spend on high fashion. The place was busy and people in the streets were carrying designer bags full of clothes. They had been spending money, big money, at the sights I saw. I could tell by the clothes they wore they were money people. It was an eye opener for me to see the affluence of Milan; there was no shortage of money here. The place was cruising, it seemed everything was selling, everybody wanted the top fashion, and a lot of the world fashion outlets were here.

The top designers were based here providing new fashion clothes for the new season. There were two seasons a year, so they were busy all year designing and manufacturing garments and accessories. I would like to be a part of that, but my focus was on one year as the face of fashion and straight into being a socialite, charging for my time as I mingled and partied my time along the way to old age. I was never going to end. At old age I would always be looking for the limelight; I was never going to grow old.

My day in Milan had shown me where I was going in life. This fashion business had no age barrier. You could be in it without realising you were getting old. I had my years ahead of me. I was here for a good time not a long time. Every day I wanted to be better than the day before -- that was my intention regardless of what was going on elsewhere. It was all about me, and I was here in this select private world of fashion. I would be instrumental to the makeup women and teenagers would wear and the hair types and cuts they would follow.

I would be a trendsetter, as they called people like me in the 60's. I was a remake of the 60's in my thinking, although I was never in love with the styles of the decades. I was only interested in today's fashion and going forward. I did not even show an interest in past fashion. I wanted to be up there, setting the standards for the future generations, not the generations gone. We were moving on into the 21st century, and we needed to move with the times like other industries and not stand still.

I had seen a lot today, in the amount of foot traffic fashion created and the passion in people to wear the best clothes and be the hight of fashion. It was a happening place and the people in the hub of it all had to look the part. Fashion was instrumental to the venue people were attracted too. I couldn't wait to be in that click of fashion icons. I would hopefully be the diva I wanted to be from a young age; it was all in my grasp now. I was more ready now than at any other time. I lived for the day. Every day was different, and it was a new experience every day. America was going to be our next destination; it was strange there was no limit on what Gino could spend. I would have just liked the difference in money between first class and baggage, as I called it.

I was not good with the cheap seats but would suffer it to save the uplift in price between the two of them. I was moving up now so it would be first class all the way from now on.

CHAPTER 19

I was having a couple of days just lounging around. It was warm, so I was in and out of the swimming pool. It was so nice to have one to escape the heat of the day. Gino had the best of everything: saunas, jacuzzi, gym, steam rooms… he was short of nothing. Everything was at his disposal, well, mine as well. He was away, so I was taking his hospitality to the max but I'm sure he would be happy with the results. Using the gym and pool had toned me up to my best level.

I was looking so good as I looked in the pools mirrors as I got out. I had to pinch myself to see if it was really me, I looked so good. I was still a young woman, but what a woman I had turned out to be, I thought. If I can't love myself, I can't love any anyone else, and I was feeling quite fidgety. Well, horny might have been a better word to describe it. Everything had been maturing, and I could feel every part of me wanted to be loved.

It wasn't for me to be a virgin bride and live with just one man. I wanted to see the world and cherry pick the best men to date. I wasn't looking for marriage, I wanted the attention from a man to enjoy him and taste his sweet kiss on my lips. I would only entertain the best in my bedroom; he would be there at my pleasure, not his. If he could get something out of it, so be it, but I was already selfish and I was not going to mellow down for no man. I was looking for a good time, not a long time. I was thirsty and he was water, just here to quench my thirst. I was not for sale, and he would never own me; I wasn't real estate, but I was real in my thinking and there was no permanent man anywhere in sight.

I would pick my man carefully; he would know when I smiled at him. It was his time to ensure all my inhibitions were taken care of. I would not be accepting any freeloaders. I wanted to see the balance of their bank account before they came into my life. No dreamers or 'the money is arriving anytime soon,' if they have nothing, I won't even tell them the time of day. What does a poor man want to know the time of day for? He can sling his hook like the rest of them. I thought I might have a cruel streak running through me, but if you had grown up where I did, you would be able to comprehend my reluctance for dreamers and conmen.

Nobody was taking me for a fool. My eyes were wide open, as I knew they would be turning up like the bad pennies they were. I was just looking forward to the helicopter ride to the airport; there would be no queuing for me at passport control. We would be like diplomats. I was hoping we would spend an hour in the executive lounge, first class, of course, nothing less would do now. Gino was my guarantee that it was luxury all the way. We would be going first thing in the morning, around 9am, ready for the flight at 11.30am to New York.

It would be around a seven-hour trip. I had a lot of things to do; I needed a book to read on the way. I found it more relaxing than watching films on a screen. I could lose myself in a good book, but it really depended on what Gino would be doing. He would get my attention before anything else. We might need to chat, as he had never said what my salary was going to be. He was looking after all my needs, so I was going to wait for him to make the first move. I didn't think the amount he offered would be up for negotiations, so I was willing to accept whatever he thought.

The job would pay a good living wage, as I was more interested in the fame than the fortune. At this moment I didn't need any money. Gino would buy me whatever I wanted, I just had to ask, and it was there. He was generous. Nothing was too much, but he had the beautiful Nigerian girl in his company, so it was reciprocal. Well, that was my take on it. I was ready for everything: the flight, New York, everything was new to me. I had to stop for a breath.

Sometimes I was so exasperated with it all. It was mind blowing to cope with all what was going on. I was running out of things to wear; I wanted to look my best but was limited to my refurbed clothes. They looked good, but the fabrics were not good, quite coarse and not good quality. I would have to ask for some new ones from Gino when we got into New York.

We sat and had dinner and a nice conversation about his family and the closeness they felt for each other. He was so lovely to chat with. I did put a word in about me needing some clothes to wear.

He replied, "I will sort it for you the moment we land in New York." I was grateful for his kindness; he was my best friend and the best I had ever had. We just seemed to bounce off each other: our conversations were interesting, and we both liked similar things. It was all sounding a bit close, but I was in control of my emotions and would not be taking our relationship to the next level. This was the next level, and I was not going to go beyond the respect we had for each other; nothing would break that bond of respect we had.

I was so happy just to be in the company of such a great man. He was so cultured, good-looking, and so caring -- he was every woman's dream. If only I had been born 25 years ago, it could have been me in place of his wife, but he was married and off the dating scene a long time ago. I wondered in my head if he had ever strayed, even for just one night of passion. It was a thought I would keep in my head forever. What kind of woman would be able to tempt him into their bed and what did he have to offer them in the bedroom?

Strange, sometimes, the way thoughts run through your head when you're close to somebody you care about. These types of thoughts are better forgotten, as my mind was in overdrive. I was a woman, after all, and women do think a lot more than men sometimes and I was definitely in that category. I would have to come back down to earth and stop floating around. My focus would be on being the face of fashion, but I was fidgety in my thoughts.

CHAPTER 20

Maybe I should just come out with it. "I love you, Gino, with all my heart. You have stolen my heart and soul, and I want to see your face lying next to me in the bedroom for the rest of our lives." I was living the dream in my daydreaming way, but it was controlled. Every girl is allowed to go off the scale sometimes just to be able to put her back on her tracks. I was overzealous with the situation I found myself in with Gino. He was a god in the fashion world, and I was his prodigy at this moment in time.

The way I was being treated, this was it, what I was looking for a generous man that cares, a rarity in my world. The men around me were looking to be the first to take away my virginity. They didn't care about my emotions. They were just looking after their own desires, and I wasn't a part of anything that they did with me. I was never going to be chased again in that way. If I was going to go beyond the boundaries I had set for myself, it was going to be because I myself was in love and it would not be lust for a man that didn't love me the way I loved him.

He would have to put his skates back on and get rolling down the sidewalk. I had no needs for a man like this; no man was going to be controlling me. I was my own person, and I only listened to people I believed I would learn something from. I wasn't going to be inviting some silver-tongued smoothie into my life when all he had was in his mouth, talking the dream to me. I already had it. What would I be receiving from someone like that was trouble.

I had the best man in the same hotel as me and no other man was going to sweet talk me into bed. I had Gino as my mentor, and I was going to listen and learn from him. If I could hold onto just a bit of his wisdom, I would be a lucky lady; he was everything I wanted to be. In my heart, I knew it would virtually be impossible to be the great man he was, but I would be trying to learn from him every step of the way. He was my destiny at a good time in my life. I would learn fast and try to be a credit to my employer who believed in me and my ability to be who I would become in the near future.

I wanted it so bad it hurt. Only time would tell how I handled the position I had been given. I was effectively an envoy for the fashion industry; we were lapping it up in the best hotel in New York, Waldorf Astoria. It had everything. We even had our own personal butler; nothing was too much to pay for Gino. He knew he was only here for a good time, not a long time, and he was going to spend his money on the luxury life he deserved. He had told me that when it was his turn to die, he wasn't going to be taking anything with him. So, he was going to enjoy what he had and would lead the life he deserved for all the hours and hard work he had put in to be where he was now.

He wasn't a greedy man but a successful man. His take on it all he was just recycling his money, and it was never his to own. He said everything was a short lease and would be dust one day. This was his time, and he was going to enjoy what he had earned. I was all up for that; he deserved it. All the money was his to spend and he had a taste for all the comforts that the good life can bring.

"Here we are," he said. "The biggest market in the world for my products. This is where it all happens," as we entered the lift in New York.

We were going to the offices; he had ten levels, he said, from the top down. The building was enormous, it was new. I had never seen a building as beautiful in my life, not even in magazines. He was the man. His empire was not large, it was humongous in size. The money it must have turned over per annum must have been extortionate. He was without a doubt the king of fashion. I couldn't imagine anyone being even close to his wealth. He had the formula for making money spot on, although he was competitive in the marketplace.

His money seemed to be justified, and his workforce were all paid the going rate. There was no slave labour in his businesses. Everything was good and everyone appeared happy to be working for International Fashion Corporation. It was a fabulous building to work in.

Gino said "yes, I like to ensure my employees are well treated and have the best pension scheme of all the fashion companies." So, they were going to be looked after at work and in retirement. "That sounds a long way off," Gino said, "but it will soon come around."

The lift pinged as we got to the top floor and the doors opened.

"Wow," I said out loud, "this is beautiful."

"Yes," Gino said. "We get that response every day." It was like being in a spaceship with the way everybody worked at their own space station desk. All the monitors were built into the desks and legless chairs; each office worker was supported off the ground in a room with a 360-degree view. It was as if I was on a spaceship, and I was about to be beamed on board, but by the looks of it I was already on board. All the desks and chairs were floating from the ceiling. This was a dream office, I wanted to work here if I had to work, but that 9-5 day would never suite me.

I was aiming to be a diva and whilst I was going to be the face of fashion for a year, I was not going to forget my goal of being a socialite and not working at all. My only workplace was going to be the gym, although looking around the vastness of the office, most of the staff were well toned. They all had the same style of dress; the men were outnumbered by the women. It seemed the women were taking the lead in design and fashion. I looked over at the monitors. It looked like most of the new designs were being invented here as they had virtual catwalk programs where they could model the clothes they had designed on a virtual catwalk.

They could change any style and catwalk the new design; it was all state of the art here. There were laptops or keypads. Everything was smart in its looks and operation. Gino had got it all down to an art. No wonder he had all the fashion houses under his control; he was a genius. This man could juggle businesses like a juggler juggling balls, he was as sharp as a pin on all business and commanded respect everywhere he went.

The security team were always within distance of him wherever we went and never let him out of their sight. He was vulnerable for kidnapping and extortion due to his phenomenal wealth and stature. Although he never said anything about them, they were just there to ensure nothing ever happened. This was probably the downside to being an entrepreneur businessman, but I couldn't wait until I needed security men.

I had never had the privilege to be wealthy. I was always the complete opposite, skint with no money. I was never going to be held for ransom. There were no reward monies coming to set me free. Sometimes, I thought it's good to have the freedom of being able to move around freely, to browse around shops looking at fashion items and nice furniture for my house in Paris, Rome, London, or Los Angeles. These were the cities I was desperate to own houses in, if I was successful.

I had been dreaming all my life, looking at places in magazines and dreaming, but my dreams were now reality.

Gino said, "We are going to Japan from here; I want to show you our stores and factories there. They're so good, and Japan is something different to any other place, it has a certain je ne sais quoi."

"What was that?" Madam Sazzar said.

"I cannot describe in detail its special distinguishing presence about it. You have to see it to appreciate the extraordinary concept of what they have achieved over hundreds of years. The place fascinates me." The next morning we were on the plane to Japan. First class, of course, darling, I was in my element.

CHAPTER 21

The Japanese were a certain race of people that had given their lives to perfection of the things that they did in their lifetime of devotion to a cause. Whatever it required, they gave their heart and soul to do our products. They are not only produced here but also made up one of our largest markets for our products. Copies that have been poorly made in other countries did not exist here; this was a place of loyalty and dignity. Nothing was too much for the people of Japan. They are meticulous in what they put their hands to; it was guaranteed to be perfect.

I could see why Gino would want to have his factory here. You could never say he could have done better. He was out there, the best in the industry, and I was so glad he was my escort. We looked around -- the factory was just a hum of sewing machines. The whole factory was buzzing. If only, I thought, I had a sewing machine, my life would have been so much easier. Here I was, though.

Maybe I might not have put the same effort into creating the designs I did in my clothes.

It was definitely a learning curve, and it was a hard lesson I would never forget. Gino paid a lot of attention to the people working on the factory floor, they were equal in their status. Men and women worked together, there was no sweatshop here. There were no children working in the factories, only adults that seemed honoured to speak to the boss. He drew so much respect from the people who worked for him. He was nothing short of their hero who provided their work in a wonderful environment and produced the best.

Gino had told me, if you want the best out of your staff look after their welfare and reward them in their pay packet, and you will always keep your staff and prosper. We spent the rest of the day in Toyoko, where we had a traditional Japanese meal. It was delicious. The fish tasted like it had just jumped out of the sea onto the plate. I could only describe the whole meal as an experience. No other word could describe it.

The way the people were, it seemed like they had been preparing their lives since the day they were born. We walked through to Bonsai tree gardens and looked at the way the buildings were constructed. The rooflines excited you as you looked up in amazement. Their attention to detail was impeccable. I was falling in love with the prospect of one day living here. Nothing ever appeared to be too much trouble, and they would bow and step back and keep bowing as they left our presence.

Gino commanded such respect from the whole of the Japanese nation. Everywhere we went, there was politeness and respect. The hospitality was second to none; it wasn't possible to improve what was already perfect. I could have stayed there for the rest of my life, but Gino wanted a new face of fashion, and I was here wanting to take on my role.

We would have to start making the right plans as time was running out for my former adversary, her year was nearly over. She was hoping to stay and be the face of fashion for the next year, but it rarely worked that way. Gino said it was a twelve-month contract and what you did would either set you up for life or destroy you if you couldn't do the job.

Gino had seen my strength and knew that I would carry it through to the end. I was no quitter, and Gino would definitely get his money's worth out of me. We would have to head back to Europe as Gino had spent time and money educating me into the business and I had learned a lot. It wasn't going to be easy to work in a woman's environment. They seemed to fall out with each other quickly, but I could handle myself. Onwards and upwards, I thought to myself, another disaster to deal with. It was all part of my days in Nigeria. The visit to Japan had been the best, it had been an experience I would never forget. These were the days to remember when I was old, rocking in my chair.

We had been in the best restaurants and tasted the finest foods in life. No place was equal in my mind, but who was I to judge. It was only my second place to visit out of Africa, but I knew class and good food. I might not have been witnessed or party to it all, but my life was changing for the better. Hopefully the past would stay in the past, and I would never have to witness poverty again.

I was on a roller coaster, and I was having the ride of my life. I hoped it would never stop. I had everything going this year and I would be working. It was nice we had taken time off before my start date, which was three days from now, at least after a long flight I would be able to chill until the first day of my work.

Madam Sazzar, face of fashion: it had a certain ring to it. I would be exploiting my face and name everywhere until everybody in the fashion industry knew it off by heart. I was hoping to be world-renown by everybody that follows fashion and one day possibly go into film as an actress. Gino had opened doors to me, doors a woman could only dream about it. It was in my head: it's who you know, not what you know.

He had opened the world for me. The world was now my oyster, and I was going to milk it to the max. Nobody would stand in my way. I wanted to be the best model in the world. I was going for it and would not give anything than my best for Gino's faith in me. Just travelling first class everywhere was more than payment for where I was going in life. How do you possibly repay a man like Gino? It would be impossible.

I wanted to be the best face of fashion he had ever employed, and he would be taking all the credit for the choice he made. He was every woman's dream, he was tall, dark, handsome, polite, and down the list filthy rich. How could my body not love him? He seemed to be a decent man, always talking about his family. He doted on them all. He was still in love with his wife after twenty-five years married. This would be the type of man I would be looking to settle with one day. He had it all going for him, and I was never going to be instrumental in dissolving what he had.

Gino was so good and would be my mentor for this year. Two days to go. I was beyond excited. Where would it lead us? He had said we would go to New York, but I think he was waiting until the fashion show was on there to come over and show me around. As long as I was travelling first class, I was happy to be on my own. Well, there would be security with me, he had told me, but it was the only way to travel now.

Would I one day be sitting there and some young woman would come into first class and knocking me off my perch? It was a long way from there, but time flies, they say. Within a few years my modelling days would be over, my main focus was the face of fashion, but I was going to take all the contacts I could make. My address book was going to have to be a large one for all those contacts. I would be having a column at the side of their names to insert their estimated wealth. The figure inserted would start in the millions.

I was not interested in armchair millionaires. I wanted to see the money and wealth, not hear about it. Anyone telling me their wealth would be crossed out immediately. I'd seen all the dreamers I ever want to see. I would always be three steps ahead of them, so it would be no good turning up at a venue to talk to me if they weren't on my list. I would not be entertaining them; they would have to show some ID and proof of who they were and what they were bringing to the party.

I wasn't going to tolerate trophy hunters or would-be's or might-be's. They would have to be people of substance, not rock climbers. I was after the people who were at the summit in life, who had reached the top in their career like Gino. He was the man who had set the benchmark for all others to follow.

CHAPTER 22

My parameters were all set at a height fools couldn't jump. It seemed a cruel statement, but where I had come from, they were climbers, the same as me, trying to find a way through poverty into a world of opportunity where we could be equal in business with the westernised people. I was going to spend a couple of nights and then I would be going for photo shoots and training in Gino's factory and modelling division.

It was going to be an eye opener, working in the fashion trade. It seemed notorious for big fallouts with other staff. I had it planned out. If they thought they were going to take me on, they needed to be bringing all their friends. I was a tiger in Nigeria and the tiger was still in here in Milan. It was a whole new world opening up for me. I had never worked as such in a job. This would be my first job and the first exposure to the fashion industry.

I didn't expect it to be a smooth one, but I had the big boss, Gino, punting for me, and I know if I didn't let him down, he would be there for me 100%. We relaxed after dinner. It was like the first night we had met. He was still the gentleman I had met in first class on the plane. He wasn't like the others who were quite brash and forward with their phone numbers. He had been polite, smiled, and said hello as he passed me standing outside the stewardess area and then meeting in the limousine outside the airport.

Tomorrow we were going into Milan. Gino was going onto Rome for a few days to see his family. He loved the children; the boys had grown so fast. He missed being with his wife, they had been best friends before they married. He had left his manager of the fashion house in Milan to look after me. It was a bit daunting, but I had to step up now. It was down to work. The holiday was over now.

It could only get better as I now needed to work for international fashion for the next year. I would hopefully meet some friends and be able to enjoy everything Milan had to offer. We said good night. The evening had gone well. Gino said he had relaxed as well going to Japan, but he was ready to go home. He described home as Rome.

Although his place was not as grand as this place in Milan, it was his home where his wife and children lived.

I would miss his company; he was a true gentleman and treated me well. This was more than I would have expected, I was never sure of what to expect, but he had shown me that nice people exist regardless of the position they held. It was installed in my head that westernised countries were not welcoming or friendly. Gino had proved different, and I was so thankful he was the first person I had real contact with. My experience was second to none.

He was the nicest man I had ever met outside my family, and it was an honour to be in his company. I was forever in his debt; I would now have twelve months to prove myself. I was nervous about going to the factory without the support of Gino. I was only just eighteen and had no experience of the job title I had taken on. It would be a complete learning curve, but I was a girl that learned fast, and I took everything in that someone told me.

I had my own take on what they might say as I had studied fashion all my life since I was very young. I was always reading about fashion and the breaking new trends. I had wanted to be here all my life, but the opportunity had never come along. It was like fate, meeting Gino and him being outside as I came out of the airport. I did wonder if he had waited for me. He must have done, as he must have thought about offering me the job on the plane coming over to Milan. I never thought to ask him why he was on a plane from Nigeria. Maybe he was scouting for new models and found one in me on my way over. He hadn't mentioned it; I was not going to ask the question. I was just happy he picked me to be his top girl.

The guards turned up just after breakfast.

"It's time to go, Madam," the guard said.

"Yes, it is," Madam Sazzar replied. "I'm ready, lead the way."

"Yes, Madam," the guard replied. I was escorted to the limousine.

"How long will the journey be?"

"About 30 minutes, Madam," the guard replied.

"Okay, I can sit back and relax then."

"Yes, Madam," the guard replied. We were on our way to Milan central; it was a comfortable ride in. I had enjoyed the ride back from the airport yesterday.

The limousine was available for my use, so I was going to make sure it was used. I wanted to see more of the city later after the induction and photo shoot. It was going to be busy; I'm sure Gino would have left clear instructions with management how to treat me and look after my welfare. They at least had the facility to feed and water me during the day; it was a concern of what I was going to meet when I got into the factory.

It seemed everything took place there; I think I would be there more than the offices. I was excited but also nervous. I kept saying to myself *I can handle everything they throw at me.* They had to know my background to realise I was not someone to be messed with. I could hold my own in Africa, so Milan would be a breeze, just a walk in the park to me. I had been bought up to be respectable but to be able to look after myself, so I had good training on etiquette and politeness, but also I had training on how to spot a traitor in the camp. I was geared up to that. There would be plenty of them here. After all, I did not fit into the European ideal.

I was African and had to work that bit harder for my place in this world of fashion, although Gino had seen my beauty and character and had taken to me. He wanted to go as far as I could, there would be no obstacles in my way. It would be all about me and my road to success. I would not be suffering any fools along the way.

CHAPTER 23

I arrived at the factory and said thank you to the guards for taking me.

"No, Madam," one said. "We will be staying here with you. The boss has said we have to be around you and not to let you out of our sight. He said we are here to ensure your safety."

I was thinking *not to worry on that one, I'm capable of looking after myself,* but Gino had got his reasons unbeknownst to me. I had come from Africa. It seemed so mild here as having to be streetwise growing up in Africa, I think he might have been over cautious but hey ho, better safe than sorry.

I was happy to have the guards around. I walked into the office with my entourage behind me, the guards. It made me feel special and cared for, someone was looking after me out there and it was Gino. He was amazingly caring, such a wonderful man and I loved him for the opportunity he had given me and the care and respect

I was receiving. It was like a dream to me. It was like I was a precious diamond, and I had to be treated with respect and security.

"Hello Madam Sazzar," the lady said as I walked into the office. "Come this way, I'm Emily. Pleased to make your acquaintance. You're very pretty."

"Thank you, that's very kind of you," Madam Sazzar replied.

"This way, Madam. We have been expecting you. Follow me please to the studio where we can formally introduce you to the staff who will be looking after you on your journey with International Fashion."

"Thank you," Madam Sazzar replied.

"I would also like to introduce you to the staff who will be looking after you and ensuring your experience here will be a good one.

"I would like to start with the face of fashion 2023/2024, Miss Chantel Peir."

"Pleased to meet you," I said, putting my hand out. She squeezed it hard; this woman wasn't happy to see anyone never mind a black girl from Africa taking her crown. I squeezed it back harder; I could see she was struggling not to squeal. I could see the look in her eyes; I had seen it lots of times before. It was one of jealousy.

I had to restrain myself. Miss Chantel would have had to see somebody about her hand, otherwise she was lucky I was on my best behaviour, or she would have been in trouble. Her time was over. She had been the face of fashion for two years running. I had knocked her off her perch, and she wasn't a happy bird. I was her replacement, and she would be history by the end of the week so I wouldn't have to be seeing her bitchy face looking at me again.

I was introduced to all the staff who would be instrumental in my modelling. They all seemed really nice. I was surprised they had put up with her for two years but hey ho it was their job to do whatever it took to make her look the way she had to for the position. She seemed like the makeup had been sculpted with a knife on her face. I wasn't being a bitch, but she was a lot older, and her face was not a natural look. I had taken over. Gino had seen the beauty in me, and she wasn't happy to see me.

I think this week was going to be a challenging one with her in the background. I wouldn't be taking any advice off her. I was a bit more streetwise than that, but I knew I was in for a week of rubbish from her. If she could have only been different, we would have had something in common, but I didn't want to even talk to her now. Whatever she said would go over my head as listening to her would be like drinking poison.

I was just 18, but 18 years of living off the streets had taught me everything I needed to know about people like her. She was not a nice person; I think she had climbed the ladder, and she wasn't happy she was on the way down. She looked like she was struggling to breathe, but I'm sure I could help her out with that. I had taken the ladder away and she was falling fast; the ground was imminent. She was going to hit it hard.

I had seen it too many times before. She was not a match for me, and I would handle anything that came to me. I would not tolerate anybody trying to undermine my intelligence, I was streetwise, and I was educated in life. Meeting her was not a good start to my new position. It was a high one, so I was going to make sure I looked after it. She would not be involved in any of it that, she could sling her hook and go. I had already witnessed what she was going to be like. She would never be a friend of mine. She could get her week finished and clear off. There was no love lost between us.

I would be looking closely at the people working with me and would be vigilant about what they were doing. I didn't want any of her friends backstabbing me, or I would have to deal with them my way and they would not like that as it wouldn't be pleasant. I had a motto: take no prisoners, and it meant what it said, this was a dog-eat-dog industry, and I was not going to give in to anybody.

I was the new current face of fashion and they'd better respect that. Anybody that didn't would be out with no second chances. I was going to sort out all the bad blood and replace it with good. I had had enough rubbish in my life and was never going to accept any. I would ensure if any came to me, they would be eating it. I was not accepting any, wherever it came from. At their peril be it, but it would not be dropping at my door.

My first experience was not good, but I think I had sent a clear message to everyone here as the jungle telegraph through Chantel was going to go around fast that I will not be intimidated by vicious people. I could see the others looking at Chantel. She was looking at the floor; she wasn't prepared to take me on. I could outlook her, outrun her, and definitely out-fight her. I was a lion in my country and not going to be pushed around.

We were over the introductions and into the makeup and what I would be wearing on our fashion photographs.

CHAPTER 24

The girls seemed more relaxed with me; I think they had two years working with an imbecile. She was in a position she didn't deserve; she was not a good person to be looking after staff with all the things models had to have done: makeup, hair, and clothes. It was a lot to do, but I saw myself as a natural woman. I would not be plastering my face with makeup.

I wanted to ensure I looked the same on camera as off. I knew sometimes I would have to wear some, but only for the light and the cameras. I was not going to encourage them to make me look like my predecessor. I wanted to look the way Gino had met me, natural in every way. I would have all my life to wear makeup, and I feared the day would come with age, but it was just a number, and I was a long way from that big number and using makeup.

It would never be a good time for me as I was more of a wash and go girl, a touch of eyeshadow and a thin line of lip gloss and I was good to go. Oh, and I nearly forgot -- always to put my heels on unless it was a beach day. I was not a plastic model; I was going to show off what my parents had made between them. I thanked the lord every day for my body and looks. I speak to my mother everyday she wasn't happy about the way I took off without a leave or goodbye, but she totally understood.

They would have talked me into staying, and I wouldn't be where I was now in life. I was going to be climbing that ladder fast and my mother and family were so excited for me and the opportunity I now had to take over the world of fashion. Every fashion house would want me, every magazine, every photographer, and every designer would want me to endorse their products.

Gino was a businessman, and if he saw an opportunity to make money, he would rent me out for photoshoots to other designers. After all, they were all in the same industry and were close in the way they all conducted business. It wasn't the dog-eat-dog industry everybody thought; they all worked well together making sure nobody was treading on each other's toes. Everybody met for functions, whether it was fashion shows or fashion awards, and everybody in fashion knew each other, it was like a big family.

I had read extensively about the fashion industry. It was much like any other. Yes, it had its moments where there were signs of copying garments and styles, but this was not patent infringements, more that most of fashion was coming back around and it had all been done before.

The makeup team wanted to connect about what I was expecting from them and what I would accept on my face in the way of oils, makeup, foundation creams, and powders. Skin was quite resilient to most beauty products so they had a clear run with what they could do, it wouldn't be doing my skin any harm. It would be something I would be monitoring over a period of time.

I went into the studio. It was the first time I would have quality makeup on my face, usually mine was what was left in the bottom of a jar in the bins from rich people. My luck once was I found one that was full, but it was the wrong colour for my skin. Now there was such a choice. It seemed there was everything there from all the leading manufacturers of beauty products. They had bought in the cases: there were five large cases with draws, surely, they would have found something to cover the face of the exiting face of fashion.

I could see why she needed all that makeup; she wasn't a pretty woman. Okay, I'm a bit of a bitch, but she deserved it. The next time I saw her I wanted it to be the last. She had a vile look about her face. The name didn't suit the way she looked at me. She never had a nice bone in that scowling face. It was about to crack, there was only the makeup stopping it. She was definitely one that would go to bed without removing her makeup. No man would want to be waking up next to her.

I was going to make sure I was always happy, as being happy would extend my looks into my twilight years. They were a long time away, but my family said they came around fast, "make sure you live your life the best you can." I heard those wise words, and I was never going to forget them, although I was going to live my life in the fast lane. I had it all sorted out now, I was on it and going to give it the best I could.

There could be no wasted time, everyday needed to be a good day with no regrets. I would be happy to be here; Gino had sorted out the visas I needed, so it was clear sailing now. I had gotten control of everything, and I was ready for twelve months of work and parties. Well, I had to make sure I was seen everywhere where the dignitaries were partying. I would be there; I was a celebrity in my own right. As long as I kept my nose clean the rest would be commonplace.

The makeup team were going to work on me. I felt suffocated when they put the foundation cream on my face. I felt like I couldn't breathe, and I wanted to get a towel and wipe it all off. I am not sure how Miss Chantel went on with it; there was nothing natural about her looks. She needed the full works before she faced the cameras, she wasn't picked for her looks. She was tall and not bad when plastered in makeup, and she had lasted longer than she should have done. She didn't look a twenty-four-month model. I could see her scowling face looking through the glass door whilst they made me up.

They were just trying out different colours and lipsticks on me, all the styles in the fashion industry. It seemed whatever they put on they took straight off. They could not find the right colour or tone; the lipstick was a nonstarter. The girls doing the lip gloss said "she is perfect. She doesn't need anything to hide her beauty; she is the most natural face of fashion we have ever seen."

I smiled. It wasn't supposed to be for my ears. They would have been putting themselves out of work if I didn't need makeup.

I said "put me some of that dark red lipstick on. If it doesn't suit me, I'm sure I will start a revolution with the men. All the men in Africa like the dark red lips, that is what women use to attract the men." When they saw that lipstick they would be on their way, it was like a drug to them. The way they used to chase after the girls, they seemed like they had never seen a diva before.

Every young woman in Africa was in love with being a socialite, that's what we lived for, the night life and the parties. Nigeria was one of the clubbing capitals in the world, though I had never really witnessed it. I was always too young, but it was my time, and I was going to enjoy myself. I wanted to make memories; I didn't want to go to my grave having never lived.

I was going to party like it was the last dance every week. I wanted to dance, but Gino was locking me away. Maybe when he was back, he might take me dancing. Not quite sure it was his thing, but it wouldn't hurt to ask. He was coming back at the weekend. Strangely enough, I was missing him. It would be nice to sit by the fire after dinner and chat about my life and his life. His was always more interesting, but I had a lot to learn, and he was the best mentor ever.

He was the god of fashion, Greek mythology lived in Gino, he was a financial wizard and a god in the fashion industry. How lucky I was to have met him. He would be asking about my progress. I would need to have something to tell him; I could not admit I had done nothing. I needed to encourage the staff to get things moving for my first week. On the following Monday, I was going to be in press meetings all week, so I needed to look good for the papers, magazines, and the news on T.V. and the internet. It was going to be a busy week; I would have to have fitting days for my clothes. The makeup was sorted; I wasn't having any. As long as the cameras were good, they wouldn't need makeup to make me look good.

I thought casual and natural was the way forward. I wanted to look the same every time a camera caught me off guard instead of looking like a horror story. I wanted to be seen and photographed with no horrendous picture in the papers or on television. I was a natural apart from the moisturising cream to keep my skin looking healthy. It was all I needed; I would be ready for the changeover. We were going to do some photos without makeup and see how they looked on the camera. We would look at the pictures in the morning. They were mainly head and neck shots, a few body ones, but I only had a few clothes Gino had given me from the factory.

CHAPTER 25

I was never going to be ready to go in the magazines like I looked now, I was too casual. I needed the best clothes that needed the best person to wear them and show off the best lines in the latest fashion. I was hoping I would boost sales once people read the magazines with me modelling the clothes and my natural looks endorsing the products. Although I would not be wearing the makeup, possibly a touch of lip gloss. I was ready for the photos in the morning. I would pick the best out of my fashion clothes, maybe I might put on a few of my handmade clothes. They could look lovely on me.

I was going back to another lonely night on my own in the mansion, but tomorrow would be another day. I was quite excited to be behind the camera; I had never been in modelling and now my face would be going worldwide. What an accolade I had won. It seemed unreal, there I was getting on a plane less than two weeks away and now I was going to be photographed for the media all over the world. I was that excited I nearly wet my pants.

I had wanted this all my life, and it was only just beginning. I was being picked up by the guards and I would be on my way home soon effectively. I was not sure how long I would be Gino's guest, but I was not in a hurry to move out. The guards were excellent and polite, and they were looking after me well. I was not sure what tomorrow would bring but I needed to relax before dinner. It would be nice to have dinner with Gino in place of being on my own there. I hoped he was enjoying his time with his family; I was really looking forward to his company again.

I was thinking that he would stay a while and see my photos after the photo shoot. I was hoping that his choice had been a good one. I was not one to disappoint anybody. I had always wanted to do my best for my employer. I hoped he would be happy with my work; it seemed like money for nothing, but I'm sure I was in for a shock at the amount of work I would be doing. It appears the things you think you will do easily always turn out to be the hardest.

I was in for a rude awakening; I would have to make sure I was up to it all. Gino was on his way; he would be here early as he had to chair a meeting of the board in Milan. I was going to do my best to get home early. If I was on the ball and listened to everything they wanted me to do, I might be able to get home in the late afternoon and be in time for dinner. Gino liked to be in the dining room for no later than 6.30pm, that way, he said, we have the night to ourselves. I was always remembering what he told me. He was like a tree full of knowledge and he was an American oak, wise in years of wisdom. He knew so much. He knew how to get in and out of different fashion, if the leaves were falling, he knew it was time to get out effectively.

If sales were poor, he looked at the stock and changed like the seasons. He always needed to be on top. He said second best was never a place to be. I listened to his wise words and took them all in. I could recite most of the things he had said. He was my mentor, my tutor, my inspiration, everything I was becoming was attributed to him. I was learning fast.

I was on my way home, reciting all his words he had said in our first days. It had all gone in and everything he had said was now a part of me. I was looking out of the limousine window, daydreaming about where my life was going now and where I would end up. I had made a good start, it's just where I finish. My life was set out for me now and I was going to have to make it work. There could be no mistakes, I couldn't afford to start all over again. This was my big start, a total one-off, and there could be no off days. Everyday had to be a good one.

I was geared up for when I got home. I saw Gino more of an adoptive parent, he was around twenty-five years my senior, so he was well in age to be my adoptive father. He treated me like a queen, but I think if he could, he would have looked at me as his adopted daughter. There could be no passion between us, as it was a professional relationship only.

I had been chatting to some of the models who told me where I would find some accommodation near the offices and factory. I was interested, as in the back of my mind was Gino, it was too much of a temptation to go with this older, wiser, groomed, tall, dark, handsome, wealthy man. What the hell was I doing leaving him in that mansion all by himself? What was I thinking would be his trouble? He was not going to stand a chance; he was discrete with his looks. He tended to glance more than having full eye contact; I swear he never knew what I was wearing from day to day.

His eyes were only on a level with mine. His eyes did wander from time to time, my fault, I suppose, as I was always putting tight clothes on my hourglass figure. I had a slim body with a peachy bum and shone out with my dark features and my posture. I was a knockout, and I think Gino realised it and was not going to take the risk, but it was in my nature to enjoy the attention of a man.

I was a virgin and, if I could choose any man to bring me into the sexual world, I would want it to be Gino. I liked older men. They had experience in life, and age was just a number. I would always sway towards the older man, as I was more comfortable around them. They made me relaxed, and I could talk to them about lots of things. They usually had the answers. They would not come and go in a heated rush but spend time getting to know me, all of me.

I was excited to have Gino in my life. He was so gentle with his words but, by using his voice, he commanded respect. As he started talking, he wasn't a shy man but a positive thinking man. He knew everything from accounting to the sizes of the models wearing the company's clothes. To show off his latest fashion, people would have thought he was effeminate, but he was all man under that mascara. He would not accept rubbish from anybody, his words were always final, and he would not let any man or woman talk him down.

What a friend I had in Gino, he was my bestie, there was no other man anywhere close to him in any form. He was clearly a one of a kind. I had some naughty dreams about him when he was at the family home, and I felt a sexual feeling for him when I was in the shower. Thoughts going through my head as I was washing my private parts, thinking about him in the shower with me, stood up with my legs astride in a form of surrender.

It was a really bad thing to have these thoughts about my boss, but it was just my age I put it down to, although I don't think it was the problem. I had become a full woman. All my monthly cycles were operating as they should and that lead me to a natural instinct to have penetration with a man. I was drawn in to older men and I fancied the pants off him. Just seeing him was enough to engage every sensor in my body. Sometimes I would need to excuse myself from the room, as the more I looked at him, the more trouble I was in.

He was like a Greek god in his looks although darker. He reminded me of Achilles, the Greek war lord Achilles, who conquered Troy. Gino had conquered me; I would have been his slave for nothing but food and love. He excited me, just to see him standing there. I was just 18 and in love with an older man. How could anybody replace him? He was on another level.

I was now into my work and next week would be my first real week working. Gino's secretary and P/R had booked me in for a photoshoot with one of the major magazines. They wanted to do a feature on me, the new face of fashion, they wanted to get it out there first. They were all waiting to meet me. I didn't know what to expect myself and what kind of reception I would get from the magazines when they saw me.

I wasn't sure whether they had encountered an African girl as the face of fashion. I was out there representing my country by being in the position I was in. I was slightly nervous, but Gino could see it in me and told me to chill, everything would be okay.

CHAPTER 26

Morning arrived, and we had a lovely breakfast spread out for us. There was so much food for the two of us, but Gino said it was always good to have a choice. He was right. There was no way my body would have taken the amount of food on Gino's plate. I was going to have to look good for the magazine pictures, it was my first photoshoot, and I had to look amazing. I didn't want to look bloated and out of shape. There could be no second chances. Everything had to be perfect first time.

There was no room for mistakes, I was not about to let anybody down, especially the boss. He said he was coming to support me; I was his prodigy, and I didn't want to let him down no matter how nervous I was. I was going to be sure I didn't let Gino down in any way, he deserved the best and he was going to get the best. I was going to play this as I had been waiting for this all my life; it was more than anybody could ask.

We got out of the limousine outside the office gates. It was no surprise that all the press were there at the gates as we were coming into the main offices. Gino told the guards to check their identity and let them into the offices. Gino was keen to get as much exposure as he could. Nothing would stand in his way. I was a money-making machine now, and I was going to do my best to ensure it all worked. It was a bit overwhelming as I got out of the car. There were so many photographers there, the light from the flashes were blinding, and I had to put my hand above my eyes to see Gino as he got out.

I saw him standing there. Photographers were everywhere. The amount of film being used must have been immense; the last time I saw lights like this was on the last night before I left Africa. It was a display of fireworks. I had never seen so many flashes. It was my turn to go out, Gino had gone first and softened the blow of all the photographers. He was so used to giving his big Oklahoma cat smile, he was in his element. He knew exactly how to keep the press interested.

I was bricking it; in two minutes it would be my turn. What kind of questions would they fire at me? The press were sometimes brutal with celebrities. They were going to make mincemeat out of me. There would be no mercy for a teenager from Africa. I'm sure that they would think I've been dragged up. I actually had some hard discipline in my life, and I knew how to respect people and treat them right. Okay, I was a taskmaster when it came to how much rubbish a person could give me, but I wasn't an open sewer waiting to take anything that was thrown down at me.

They would have to treat me with the respect I deserved. I was just a minute away from Gino introducing me. I looked from behind the curtain. It was full. It seemed they all had tripods and single cameras, it was going to be hell out there and I was about to be called out. I was feeling my stools were loose and I didn't know if I should go to the toilet or face the press.

It was going to have to be the press as I had no time to go to the toilet. I said to myself *pull yourself together. You're Madam Sazzar, the biggest diva in the world. You're going to take the world by storm.* I breathed a sigh of relief, and I was ready. Gino opened the curtain, took me by the hand, and walked me out. The press put their cameras down in amazement and all started clapping, they carried on for what seemed like minutes, and I was overcome with emotion.

I managed to pull myself together as I didn't want to look weak. I needed to be strong and show them all I was in control of the position I was going to hold. I smiled and the press went wild clapping and cheering; I had won the crowd, and that was a big achievement for Gino. He was smiling, his pearly white teeth glistening as the cameras flashed. He was reeling in it; I was his prodigy, and I was coming through for him.

Gino calmed the photographers down and said "okay, let's take it easy" in his English Italian accent. I listened to him talking. I was getting excited; this was my man talking well. I thought of him as my man, he was my boss, but who doesn't fancy a good-looking boss? If you don't like the looks, the money is always a bonus, but I had the best-looking Italian man ever. He was a Greek god from Italy, and he was my boss but also my friend. The lights were blinding from the photography; they really liked me.

I was in an outfit I had made myself. Gino said he would use me for his latest fashion collection. He said I was really talented, better than most of his designers. He said he would always have a job if I didn't take to being the face of fashion, fat chance of giving that up. I thought, *that's never going to happen.* I needed that platform to leap into what I wanted to be. Gino had given me the opportunity to go to the top of the ladder; nothing was going to stop me getting there.

The press loved me, and I was so relieved they did. I had been on my best behaviour, and I was now relaxed and ready for all the questions they would fire at me. The cameras flashes were constantly going; it was a bit intense for my eyes. I had never been used to it, but I thought to myself, *this is how it's going to be in fashion.* I had got my share of the limelight already, and I was having second thoughts, but I was into fashion now, so I had to know what to expect.

The questions started to come to me.

"Where are you from?"

"Do you speak Italian?" one reporter said.

"No, I only speak English, Hausa, and Yoruba, but English is my natural language."

Another reporter asked, "have you worked in fashion before?"

"Yes," I replied. "I used to design and make my own clothes."

"Excuse me," the press man replied, "did you design the dress you're wearing?"

"Yes," I said "I did it all."

"It's a beautiful outfit, who made it dare I ask?"

"Yes," I replied. "I made it."

"What?" he said. "You designed it and made it?"

"Yes," she said.

"Absolutely fabulous, it looks so good on camera, you are an amazingly beautiful woman."

"Thank you."

The press all started taking photos again but of me. I stood up and they were snapping away like I was rotating. The outfit was short, showing off my long slender legs and my pearl high heal shoes. Gino had approved my outfit, and the press loved it, to them it was high fashion. Definitely suited to the girl who was the face of fashion. I had worn the right outfit; the press loved it. I had made it to look sexy, and it had made its impact on the press and Gino. He wanted me to design clothes for him after the year was out. I was a bit sceptical of not being too tied down to working, designing clothes.

I was not going to be doing anything apart from what I was employed for. It sounded like too much work for me. I was going to be a face of fashion, and I would be moving on to my favourite place, North America. I was going to take over their fashion industry with my looks and ability to provide the right production in the right place. I saw myself as the right production. All I had to do was find the right place. America was a golden opportunity to spread my wings. After living in Africa, America would be a breeze.

More cameras were still flashing away when Gino ended the session. I was quite happy. I had found my feet, and I was ready for whatever was thrown at me. I had gained my confidence, and nothing was going to stop me. I was on a roll and going for it. Nobody would put down the adrenaline that was inside me, it was bursting out of me. I was not going to lose my momentum. It was moving so fast I wondered if I could keep up with it. I needed to take some chill time to evaluate my position.

I was only just starting out at a permanent job; I had to give value for money or be out of a job. I was ready to get out there and prove to the world I was worthy of the position I held. The press was outside the factory waiting for us to come out. Gino said, "it's because you're new and they want to get a full profile on what you do and where you come from. Just tell them the truth and it will set you free." I always learned that.

They were invited in, and I spoke for 90 minutes, telling them all about my life. Gino was impressed with all my answers, and he showed his approval by smiling as I was giving the press the answers. I had passed with flying colours at the moment; I was not over the bridge yet. I could see that the still waters could turn to rapids at any moment. I would have to make sure I kept up my etiquette and made sure all my words ran in sync with each other. They were still firing questions; I couldn't afford to stutter or go quiet. I had to be fully professional in my career as a diva.

I would be having to stand up and talk at large parties in the future. That's where my life was going to be going. This should be just a walk in the park for me, all I had to do was answer the rest of the questions right. I was thinking, *what if they ask me things I don't know yet?* Gino had already covered that in a no comment answer.

It was a good answer to a question, as it seemed to stall the conversation whilst the press was writing it down and putting it through for a comment to re-address somewhere in the future, which gave us time to project the right answer to the question asked.

CHAPTER 27

I was not going to be quizzed every time I posed for the cameras in the way I had been today. It would have to get easier the more exposure I had to the press meetings. I was nearly out of here, I could see Gino stepping over to rescue me from the piranhas.

"Okay, thank you," he said in a toned voice. It was as smooth as silk. They all got up off the floor where they had been sitting, most of the press getting a better view with the cameras. They clapped again, which was my queue to move off and wave as I left.

They were still taking pictures as I left the room. I had learned today that I wasn't camera shy and I could hold my own during question time with the press. I was on a bit of a roll, and I was excited. All I needed was a good kiss off Gino and an evening in Gino's room. Ha well, that was not going to happen, but my body was responding to his persona.

He was everything a woman that liked older men would crave to have. The way he dressed was impeccable, he had a presence about him. He turned me on; I had to behave myself as I could see trouble on the horizon and the trouble was me. I had made that promise, and I could not go against my instincts, but could I overrule it by my desire to have his body next to mine naked in his bed? The thought was too much. I had to look away and pinch myself to make sure I wasn't going to do that. It would put me in an awkward position.

I would be looking for a cardboard cutout of him for the bedroom, that would cause a stir around the staff. It was probably not a good idea, but it would keep me away from the real thing. Gino, I was sure (and it might be a woman's intuition but, if I put my mind to it, I was sure), would be mine, but that would be me biting the hand that fed me. It didn't do me any harm dreaming, if only I could find a man like Gino. Someone so in command of what he did I bet he had never tripped over in his whole life.

He was too sure footed and careful in everything he did, all calculated but that was probably the way the business worked. He had told me it wasn't always the way its perceived to be now. I promised myself to clear my head of all my thoughts, and it was time to focus on the job in hand as the face of fashion.

I couldn't wait to read what the magazines would be saying about me and how good the photographs would come out. They had to be good; it wouldn't go down to well if I turned out not to be photogenic and I looked awful on the photographs. We said goodnight. Gino had a cigar standing next to the fireplace, surveying all he owned.

He liked this place better than home; he said he felt calm here and was never hurried and he felt at peace in his life. It's strange how you sometimes only remember certain things that people tell you, like you filter bits out. I think Gino would have called it selective memory; he said he had come across a lot of people with that condition.

It was time to put the memory back to sleep. I had a big day tomorrow. I had done all the basic training. All I had to do was put it into practice what I had learned. At least that bitch of the exiting face of fashion hadn't shown her face. Gino had not given her chance to do a third year; he could probably see the change in her persona. She was not a nice, approachable woman but quite sour and very troublesome in her manner.

I was glad she was not nice; I would have felt bad taking her place otherwise, but I was glad I was the one taking over her place. She was out of it; she was ugly in her face when she was scowling and that was most of the time when she was looking at me. It was my age more than anything, as no matter how good you look you can't turn back the clock. Her scowling face showed that, but I was not your average 18-year-old girl. I was a fighter. I had to fight for everything I had and nobody like her was going to take away my crown.

It belonged to me now and it was history for her; she was ready to sling her hook and move on. She wasn't inundated with offers, so she was just a run of the mill model, you see girls like her every day. She had nothing I would have liked to steal off her, either looks or body, apart from the crown she reluctantly had to pass down to me. The way she looked, I thought she was going to throw it when Gino asked her to remove it.

I was so young to be here in this, one of the best jobs in the world. All I had to do was dress up and look good for the photos. They wouldn't have to ask me to smile, I was going to always be smiling. How could I not smile? I had everything to be happy with. I knew I would be meeting some rubbish along the way with being so young, but I was a woman with a body of an 18-year-old and the mind and experience of a 30-year-old. No one was going to piss on my fire. It was going to keep my life warm for the next year.

Gino had been a bit coy in telling me what my income would be. He said I needed a management company to look after it for me as it would be a substantial amount. $100 was a substantial amount of money to me with what I was used to. Gino had already given me funds to keep me going, but I hadn't spent any of it. I was still on my original $100 I bought from Africa.

I wasn't in need of anything. Gino had taken care of everything, and I could never thank him enough. It was late, my mind was on overdrive, and I needed to count sheep to get me some sleeping hours done. Tomorrow was going to be proper work, no more fairy tales. This was it. I was now in work and was going to have to earn my money.

I dropped off fast and before I knew it, the sun was coming through the window; it was getting close to my phone alarm going off. It was morning. I had 20 minutes before it went off. I was wondering whether to have the 20 minutes reading messages on my phone from my friends in Nigeria or try to have a cat nap for 20 minutes.

I was looking at my phone and the next thing the phone was going off. I had drifted back to sleep.

It was a good job I hadn't turned the alarm off, or I would have woken up late for work and Gino would not have approved of my lazy head. I needed to be professional in my approach to my new position. I was up there, right at the top; I had been catapulted from chancer to a top position. I thanked God Gino had been there that day on the plane; he had changed my life completely. I was a different person now; I was no longer the poor girl who used to be obscure, making clothes out of castaways.

CHAPTER 28

I was now going to be the best fashion had to offer. There would be no more second-hand clothes and shoes, only the best would now be there for me to wear to show off my beauty. I was going for it. I was excited to go to work, and what a job I was doing. Most people hated work in Africa; I was loving every minute of it. Gino was ready to work, so I finished off my breakfast and walked outside to the car.

We had a change of drivers. Gino was trying to explain where we were going to the new drivers. They seemed to know the area, and we were good to go. Gino was explaining what the work would entail today. It would be a mix of cat-walking clothes and shoes and facial pictures for makeup etc. Just a taste of what was coming. I had no experience cat-walking, but I was a fast learner.

I didn't want to look like a camel with a broken leg going down the catwalk. I needed to be the best; I needed that accolade of being the best catwalk model ever. I said I would like to go last on the catwalk. I didn't want Gino to know I was a total novice at everything. I wanted him to know he had found the best. I learned more in the thirty minutes than I think I had learned in my whole life. It seemed that way, but I was ready for it.

I was dressed up and ready to walk; I had some figure-hugging clothes on: a pair of cream leggings with a slight flare at the bottom and a two-belt top. The style was so good, and it fit me like a glove. I was wearing a white blouse with silver ribbon sewn in vertical lines with a brown silk collar shimmering in the lights of the catwalk. I had five-inch stiletto heels on brown short, pointed boots.

I looked a million dollars as I started to walk. I was a natural in stilettos as my sister used to have them in her wardrobe on the island in Lagos. When I went to babysit my niece, I would always be walking everywhere, cat-walking in her boots. She tried my favourite boots on as she was going to a ball, and she needed to match with her dress. She was complaining to her husband about the quality of the boots, if only she knew I had worn them out. All those months of babysitting paid off; I was the best cat-walker of all of us; they were all clapping for me as I exited the stage.

It had been a good walk; Gino's eyes were nearly popping out. I caught him looking as I turned to go into the dressing room; he was hooked today. I had done what I set out to do. Gino was under the spell of a really special woman, and there was no way back for him. He was on the hook. All I had to do, when I was ready, was reel him in and put him in the net until I was ready for him.

I had become one of the most sought-after women in the world. I was starting to earn my title; Gino had picked well but had also bought his demise. I would never let it go to the next stage and break up his marriage. I said and promised that would never happen. It wouldn't stop me showing him as much attention as I could. I would be walking arm in arm with him. I wanted the world to know he was my mentor, and he had seen more in me in months than people had seen in years. I wanted to be his best friend; I would never call him ever; he was my bestie.

If I thought he was wrong, he would always be right. He knew everything. I couldn't wait to show him all the love I could, but I would never be his wife or mistress. Definitely his best friend. I would always be there for him the way he was for me. I would live an eternity as his friend; he was everything I ever dreamed about, but dreams don't always come true. We can only live in reality, and dreams were very few for the majority. I had been given my dream by my best friend; I was so grateful to him.

I was ready for home; well, the mansion. It was at this moment in time Gino said I would be travelling a lot and meeting lots of dignitaries. I whispered under my breath "that's great. My diary will soon be full of all the richest people in the world." I was imaging all the parties I would be invited to; my telephone number would be everywhere in the world, ready for invitations to flood in.

Everybody would be waiting to be seen with the face of fashion. I was so different from the last scowling bitch; nobody would have invited her. Just her face would kill the atmosphere of any party. She was not a good envoy for fashion and Gino's empire. I was a million miles away from her in beauty and character. It was good riddance to bad rubbish; she had gone and would never return again whilst I was here.

I would be protecting my own interests and Gino's; she must have damaged his business as she was not a good person. *Oh well onwards and upwards*, I thought to myself. *I'm at a higher level now than she would ever reach.* I came out of the dressing room; Gino had gone but left a message with the driver and security that he was still in the building but where, nobody knew.

The office girls bought me some food and drinks, but it was not for me. I was never going to be a champagne girl. I didn't like the taste of alcohol and the results of drinking it. I was safe with fresh orange juice and water; I was used to making my own due to oranges being a sustainable fruit. The food was healthy in Africa, I had salad in place of the pasta and pizza – that was not for me, all that would go straight on my rear. I needed to ensure it was the most photographed rear ever.

I sat there eating, thinking about my family and what they were doing. As soon as I had the money, I would invite them over and show them where I had come in such a short time. I was hoping they would be so proud of me; I was daydreaming and woke up as Gino was on his way towards me. I was glad to see him, and I let him know with a big smile. I wanted to throw my arms around him and kiss him, but I knew that wouldn't be a good idea, especially at his workplace. That would have put the cat among the pigeons.

He apologised for the time away; I was happy as I had had time to reflect on all the important things in my life I needed to address and not walk away and forget. I wasn't wanting to go back to Africa, but I loved all my family and missed them. I was ready to find out exactly what I was worth salary-wise as the face of fashion. Gino confirmed he would let me know before the weekend, three days to go.

I thought I was excited; I was trying to guess in my head, but I had no idea how much the position paid. I had it in my wildest dreams that I would be a millionaire before I died and I was going to spend my life trying to earn my million. They were just dreams; the $100 note was a dream to me, and that's why I would find it wrong to part with it. $100 the only money I had ever had in my life. I had saved so long and sewed so many clothes, there was no way I would ever be poor again. It would not be leaving my purse; I didn't know what was older, the purse or the $100 note.

Gino said, "I have something to tell you, but I will tell you over dinner tonight. I'm taking you out to my favourite restaurant, and I want to show you off to my competitors out there. I need you to go into the dressing room and pick anything you want to wear; I know you're going to make me proud to have chosen you for the position you hold." The staff were all still there as I went in; Gino had told them to get ready for my coming back.

I came out twenty minutes later. Gino had been having a coffee and chilling. He had a plan but wasn't going to tell her until dinner.

I came over to Gino from behind. Gino turned around.

"Wow," he said, thinking she looked like a princess from another world. She was possessed by beauty; she was absolutely stunning. Gino stood up kissed me on her cheeks and took out his handkerchief. Wiping away the tears, he said "your beauty is unparalleled. I've never seen such a beautiful woman ever, you are amazingly gorgeous, you are every man's dream. There is no comparison out there to you, I wouldn't swap that day on the plane for anything in the world.

"We are going to sell so much on the sales from you and your beauty, which is incomprehensible. You're a total one-off, never to be replaced in all the years of fashion. I've never had the pleasure of someone as wonderful as you, you're a credit to my whole business empire. It was a good day meeting you, Madam Sazzar. I'm sorry I was just overcome with my emotions; you're the daughter I never had, and I'm sure she would have been as beautiful as you are. I really wanted one, but we had the second boy, and the doctors said she would never be able to carry another as her body would never go the full term of pregnancy."

I felt sad for Gino. He really wanted a girl, and I felt I was becoming more like his daughter than his lover. I was happy to be the daughter he never had. Although my skin was a different colour, my personality and caring nature were making him think I was the daughter he never had. I wouldn't mind sharing my love between him and my real parents. After all, he was looking after me like a father.

CHAPTER 29

I wonder that day on the plane and in the car outside the airport if he saw me as a daughter in place of an employee. We had become so close, and he had kept his distance from becoming anything else. That had all been in my mind, not his. I was so glad I never tried to take it to the next level, as that could have ruined my career. I certainly would not be the face of fashion 2024-2025. It was obvious he saw my beauty in his unconceived baby girl. It was so cruel, I felt for him.

He was taking me to his favourite restaurant, and I was getting excited.

He said, "good, I can see you are ready. Let's go. They are expecting us." I linked arms with him, and I felt him squeeze my hand. It was such a loving thing to do. Although I was really young, he was protecting me from anything that might turn up that's bad. I felt safe and tightened up our arms, pulling myself in closer to him. He was so handsome, I didn't care whether he loved me as a daughter or lover anything I would accept from him. He was my mentor and possibly my stepfather, only time would tell.

As I got older and more acceptable as a girlfriend my infatuation towards him could turn out to be platonic and not real. He was although older, the most attractive man I had ever had the pleasure to know. Somehow, I was attracted to his olive skin and his voice speaking Italian and English Italian. His voice was soft and silky smooth. I had just cut our relationship; it was never going to be anything beyond what it was now.

He would always be my favourite man. Nobody had what he had to be able to take his place, but he was mine for now and I loved it. He was a gentleman, opening doors whether getting out or in the offices. He always went ahead like he was about to introduce his daughter.

We were at the restaurant, and the guards let us out the car. They were very polite as they opened the doors, and they were very protective, looking around to make sure it was safe to exit the car. It was a safe place to be. Gino had told me they were bullet proof and the best place to be in the event of an attack. He had taken all necessary steps to ensure his safety and the safety of any passengers like me.

I felt so safe around him, he was my rock, and I was so glad to have him in my life. We got into the building where the restaurant was. It was like a large skyscraper you would usually see offices in. It was on the top floor, about forty storeys high, the lift, as we got in, was all chrome and mirrors. It was beautiful. I could have spent all day in it going up and down. If this was the lift, what on earth was the restaurant going to look like?

There were two men on the door as we rounded the corner, and, as we got closer, they opened the doors. It was something I had never seen before. There was so many people in the place. It looked like volcanic rock on the walls, with fire and lava flowing down the walls. It was obviously not molten rock, but at first glance it looked like it. On some of the walls, there were fish tanks from floor to ceiling. It was amazing. The amount of large colourful fish there was in the tanks – how could this be? The weight alone should have made the building collapse; Gino had done well here.

He asked if he could leave me to go to the bathroom and just circulate on the way there. He went to nearly every table where everybody there stood up and shook his hand. He was his own celebrity here, he was the man, and everybody seemed to like him and were very polite.

Some of the ladies curtsied in his presence. Gino was the top of his profession; I enjoyed watching him as he spoke to all his friends and business colleagues.

I could see he eventually got to the toilet door; well, I assumed it was. I would never see him again if he entered a second dining area. I was just chilling; a waiter had passed with a tray of champagne flutes full of that sparkling wine people pay a fortune for. I had never actually tasted it, but I was going to grab one as he passed by again. Gino was out and came over to me, pointing out the fish and telling me the species of fish they were. He seemed to know everything about anything.

"Let's go over to the table, Madam Sazzar," he said, stopping along the way and introducing me to all the people as he passed the tables. Some of the ladies were nice and asked me some questions and greeted me nicely, whereas some were so far up their own bottoms, they could not see the writing on the wall. I was the face of fashion, and it was something they would have to face. 18 years old was a long time ago for many of the ladies in here. They would have to understand this was my time now; theirs had been and gone.

I was now the new girl on the block, and I was here to stay. No woman would try to drive me away with a scowling face, I was taking no rubbish here. They were just people like me, and I wasn't about to accept any poison they were going to throw at me with their tongues as slippery as they were. Talking in riddles to hide their hate for me they were feeling inside when they saw me. There was no need for their attitude. I had done nothing but say hello for the first time.

I could see half of them were smiling and half were scowling behind the cover of their husbands or friends, but I had caused a stir, and I was happy. It was strange all the people in Africa were happy, even my family, as poor as we had been, we were all happy. I wanted to live my life. If it was going to be like this all the time, I thought I would be better going back to Africa.

I had too far to go back and Gino was going to tell me what the company would be paying for my services tonight as promised. I think he was waiting for the right time to tell me; they were in hard times and the salary would have to be in line with a declining marketplace for fashion. I had just arrived at the wrong time, and it was going to be limited.

If I could get $10,000 per year, it would be $10,000 more than I earned in Africa. I was a bit nervous. $10,000 was a lot of money, but I would be travelling and seeing lots of nice places and living in 5-star hotels, not bad for a recycled fashion designer from Africa. I was up there with the rest of them around us, up to $10,000 a year. I felt like a queen.

"Let's sit down," Gino said, as I was standing at the table with everybody wondering why I couldn't sit down.

I don't think they had any idea how rich I was going to be soon. What would I do with all the money? I couldn't keep it in my bag, imagine all that money in my bag. It would weigh so much. I would have enough to make clothes out of it. Imagine that, walking down the road in a dress made out of American dollars. That's where I was going to end my days as a socialite, it was the happening place. Beverley hills that's where I wanted to be when I was settled in as a diva.

It would be parties every night, but I thought to myself, *by the time I have made a million I will be an old lady with a walking stick. Nobody will be interesting in taking me out and paying for dinner.* I would have to spend my money taking them out. Maybe I should just go back to Africa and see if I could find a rich man like my sister and live on the island in Lagos.

I was daydreaming again. I could hear somebody talking. It was Gino, asking me to sit down. I had been daydreaming and lost all contact with the world. I was somewhere else. I apologised and sat down. The table was set for a four-course meal, as I counted the knives and forks and we had four of each. It didn't mean we had to eat four courses. I had to think of my figure. I could never lose it, and I would be a bouncing baby girl. The face of fashion needed to be perfect in every way and be able to be pliable to fit into tight clothes and look amazing.

I was here to show off the fashion Gino's designers put me into to get the best out of the clothes. I looked amazing standing there; I didn't want to sit down. I had an audience of men and women staring at me whilst I was standing. I had to sit down before I had every man in the restaurant in trouble with their wives or partners. I was stealing the show. There was no room for second best; the floor was all mine.

CHAPTER 30

I sat down, as I could see Gino getting a bit fidgety with me as I was taking all the attention away from the other guests, but these were Gino's friends. I had to remember not to show him up. I was more his daughter than his lover, and people could see there was no love connection between us. It was now platonic, and I would be having to act like the position I had been given. It was the fault of the staff in the dressing room who had given me clothes that were body hugging tightly.

I looked around. Most of the women were in dresses and power-dressed in trouser suits. They were obviously businesswomen, possibly working in the industry or in magazines. They looked like the girls in all the mags I used to read, all out of date but still showing what the staff and the models wore. I was here now. I was the one everybody was looking at. It looked like the clothes had been shrink wrapped on me with a hair dryer, but I felt good in them. You know what they say: if you've got it flaunt it, and I was doing my best to attract attention.

Possibly the wrong attention, but they were all fair game for my diva days to come. I would be ready to be taking a few cards off some of the men for keepsakes, as I know they would be my clients and I would be the one to chaperone them to dinners, dances, parties etc. If they had the money, I would be there, relieving them of some of it. I wasn't going to be greedy as long as I was up there by the time I was fifty.

I would have had a good innings, as they say in cricket. There was a thought: plenty of rich men like and support cricket. There was another avenue for me to explore, but I could see the waiter coming over, so I focused on Gino. He still had his head in the menu, looking at the specials for this evening. I could see all eyes were on our table. I was wondering, were they looking at me or Gino?

I had to look at the menu, I was starving for some food. I was also starving for the right man to come along. There were four seats around our round table. Gino said we could have a starter until our guests arrived.

"Guests?" I said in a questionary voice.

"Yes, I have a surprise for you. They should be here at any time." The waiter opened a bottle of champagne and started to pour it into the flute glasses.

"Wow." It was so good and smooth as it went down. This wasn't the prosecco I had been used to having the odd glass of at my sister's house. I used to empty all the glasses of champagne into one from people leaving, some not drunk, and I would put it all in a bigger glass and hide it in the back of the refrigerator. Well, I tell people I don't drink unless it's in my face, then I will have a glass.

I sneaked a drink of it most nights until it was gone so although I never drank or purchased alcohol, I didn't mind finishing off the leftovers from the party glasses. I hadn't obtained a taste for champagne. It tasted nothing like this champagne I was drinking now. I raised the glass to Gino.

"Good health and happiness to you, Sazzar, I hope."

And as he said that I heard, "hello father." I looked behind me. Well, I beg you not there was two of the best-looking teenage boys I had ever seen.

They said 'father.' These were Gino's boys. What on earth were they doing here?

"Sit down, boys," Gino said in English. I bet they only spoke Italian as they sat down. I looked at them individually. One looked about 15 and one about 17. Gino introduced them.

"This is Enzo, and this is my oldest boy, Marco. Boys, this is Madam Sazzar."

"Hello," the oldest boy said in perfect English.

"Oh, lovely to meet you, Marco."

"It so nice to meet you at last. I've heard so much about you from Father. What he said was right: you are beautiful."

The youngest boy, Enzo, said, "Yes, I will second that you are absolutely fabulous."

Wow, I thought. *This boy is a bit above his age. 'Absolutely fabulous.' I would expect a comment like that off Gino.* The waiter turned up for the order, he stood there whilst the boys were looking at the menu.

Gino said, "just pick your starters, boys, as we are hungry and we need to eat."

"Yes, we are too," Enzo replied.

"I could eat a horse," madam Sazzar said. "I know what I would like, the prawn salad. It sounds really nice." Gino said to the waiter "make that two." The boys both said they wanted crab and lobster pate with garden salad.

"Oh," Gino said, "are you sure?"

I thought to myself, *they're trying to keep up with me.* The 17-year-old had not taken his eyes off me and my figure since he was standing at the table when I first saw him. He was being hypnotised by me; I wondered if he had ever had a girlfriend yet. He was really handsome, like his father. The apple had fallen off in the right places with his two boys. They were going to carry their fathers looks. They were young, but I could see the potential in them both.

Enzo was developing a lust for women, well one only, at the moment: me. His eyes were transfixed on me; he was not even bothered by what anybody else was thinking. People were turning around to look at us. Marco was looking around the tables. Who was he looking for? Gino had his head in the new menu. I didn't see anything, but Marco started a silly cough to get his attention back on the table.

I was hot enough to handle anything that would come from Enzo. I saw Gino's face appear over the top of the menu. It was Enzo's cue to take his eyes off me. If Gino had known, he would never have invited them. He was going to discuss my money. I didn't want him to discuss it in front of his children; one was only one year younger than me, but I was not going to be entertaining a child.

I had an eye on his father, not a youngster. Although he was handsome, he was not for me. Give me the older men any day, they know how to treat a woman and that's what I'm looking for. I hadn't come all this way from Africa to be funding my own entertainment. I was counting my blessings that he wasn't any older. My hormones were all over the place at the moment, and I didn't want to be making any decisions on a relationship.

He wouldn't be here for me but for himself. He would struggle to support himself, never mind me. My train wouldn't be carrying unpaid passengers; he would have to grow up a bit first, and I wouldn't think Gino would like it if his son Enzo was involved with his employees. His top employee. I had to protect my interest in the company and be professional, whatever my cravings.

My hormones were relaying to me it was going to be overruled by that item between my ears and not what was between my legs.

CHAPTER 31

I had a business to build on and needed the capital behind me to do it. Gino said he had just invited them to meet me here rather than at work as the boys were still at school. I was glad they weren't going to stay that long, as I needed to be able to chat to Gino about the salary, and I was a little uncomfortable. Every time Gino was distracted by someone waving from another table or waiter filling up drinks and taking orders, Enzo's eyes were piercing and getting into the back of mine. Had he never seen a nice-looking African girl before? His eyes were nearly out. After all I had made the right entrance and looked stunningly beautiful.

I was hoping I might get about $2,000 a year. If I looked the part $12,000 a year. I would be happy with that. Just the thought of all that money would keep the men away. It was my money, and no man was going to steal it away from me. I had a good upbringing. We were always honest and, even though we were poor, theft was never in our remit. We were poor, but at least we were honest. My world was my oyster, and I was going to milk it all to the max.

Dinner was nearly over; Gino had excused himself to go and circulate around the people at the tables. He was sitting, having a coffee with two couples whilst I was babysitting the boys. I didn't know where to put my face. I was blushing. It was a good job my skin was dark, or Gino would have picked up on it. They were not going to get away with staring me out. I wasn't sure if it was lust from Enzo or if it was because that his dad was out with me. He wasn't aware it was just business tonight; I think he was being overprotective of his dad and looking after his mother's best interests.

He was probably thinking it was me he was after; it could have been 'daddy is not to be trusted,' although Gino had asked them to come, and he was excited to show me to the world. So, I would see if anything developed that would change my thoughts on Enzo and Marco. They were nice, well-educated boys, but that's what they were. Frankly, they were not men. I could handle a man, but what could I do with boys apart from babysit them to make sure they were not falling out?

I tried to be the first to make a conversation, and I asked about the education they were having and if they liked doing the work needed to complete the course. They were very polite, but I had an idea Enzo was still searching for something. His eyes felt like they were in the back of mine, looking for some kind of message he could show his mother when they got home.

I felt a bit for Gino's wife, as she had two lovely boys, but the industry Gino worked in was mainly girls and not so many men. They were probably reporting back to mother – or was this just me being horrible, looking after my own interests? Gino was at last making his way back to the table. The boys were quite polite and said it was nice to meet me and wished me luck as the face of fashion.

Enzo said I deserved the chance to go for it, as I was very attractive. That was a shock, as I thought he did not like me. I thought his thinking was that I was going to take his father away from the family. They had no need to worry, well, okay no need at the moment. He was so desirable as a man and every woman would have loved the opportunity to go out with him.

Gino said, "are you ready boys? The car is waiting to take you back. I still have some unfinished business to do here with Madam Sazzar."

"Thank you for the meal, Father," they said more or less together.

"My pleasure, boys. I will see you back at the house." They were staying with us at the house. *That will be nice; I will try to get to know them more when we're back.*

The boys were met at the door by our drivers and bodyguards; they waved goodbye, and we waved back.

"Right," Gino said. "Your salary." I got all nervous. This was it. I could feel my face beginning to get hot, and I was trembling slightly. I think Gino picked up on it. As we were about to talk, the waiter bought over a bottle of champagne and flute glasses. It was going to be a celebration.

I felt an easing in me as I was half thinking this could be the end of my career before it started.

"Well, my dear," he started as the waiter popped the champagne cork and poured the champagne into the glasses. I sat there, waiting for him to say something. He got his pocket book out and wrote something on it then passed me the paper he had written on. "I hope this meets with your approval."

"I hope so," Madam Sazzar said, taking the piece of paper. $25,000. I was nearly crying, holding back the tears that were coming into my eyes.

"That's so generous of you," I said.

"Yes, it's only the start. What will you do with your money?" he said. "We always pay in dollars, as the main company is registered in America and its easier for us to transfer monies without having to do a transfer and currency change."

Madam Sazzar said, "thank you. $25,000 is a lot of money."

"$25,000?" Gino replied. He said, "it's $250,000." Madam Sazzar stood up to see it properly in the light and said, "I have to sit down. I feel lightheaded."

Gino said, "well, it's the right money for the job, and you will definitely earn it."

"Yes," I said. "I can't believe it; I can buy my mother and father a nice house to live in and still have enough for myself."

"Don't you worry, this isn't the end. You will also get appearance bonuses throughout the year, which could give you the same again."

"What?" I was confused. "Another $25,000?"

"No," he said, laughing, "another $250,000.

"You're at the top of what you are going to be doing. You do everything so well we all decided we should pay you the whole salary, as you are not a trainee. You walk fabulously, you look fabulous, and you're really well-spoken, so much better than your predecessor."

A smile came over my face.

"Thank you," I said. "I couldn't wish for a better boss and friend than you. I really appreciate what you have done for me, and I will never forget it." I was crying.

Gino took his handkerchief out of his pocket and said, "dry your eyes dear, we don't want you all upset."

Madam Sazzar said, "I'm not upset. I'm so grateful for your support; you're such a generous and kind man."

Gino said, "it's just business with a bit of pleasure. You will earn your money, nothing comes easy."

"Yes," Madam Sazzar said, "I will, you will see. I will work harder than anybody else. I appreciate everything you have done for me since I boarded the plane in Nigeria, you have been my guiding light, and I am so grateful."

Gino said, "you will be able to pay me back, as you're going to be earning a lot of money for the business with your looks and figure. Everybody likes you, and you will be a famous lady by the end of the year. I would like to have been instrumental in helping you on this path to fame."

"Thank you," Madam Sazzar blurted out. I was so excited, thinking about the long stop, up to 500 thousand a year. I would be cruising, worth a million dollars in two years. I had my dream fast forwarded by forty-five years. I was going to be so well off and nobody's puppet anymore.

I was going to soon be a millionaire, and I would be able to do all I wanted to do and be the person I had dreamed of, a socialite, a diva. I would now have my dream. Just two years of being the face of fashion, and I would be free. America was my dream place. I always wanted to go there; I was going to be a socialite there. This was where all the money was and was spent on parties. I didn't want to host one, I wanted to be invited to them all.

They would never be paying for anything; it would all be coming free. I might decide just to stay in fashion for a while. I was top in my job, and I could probably pick up some phone numbers from here. I needed to have a full social life, and a full telephone diary, before I left international fashion and Gino, he would be the first person I would miss, but it would be an adventure into the unknown. I could handle anything this world could throw at me; America was the richest country in the world to live in, so I was going to make sure I lived the best possible life there.

With a full diary and only being twenty years old, the world was my oyster. I was sure that if I got through these two years, I would be good to go. Gino said he was going to do a two-year contract with a six-month trial period. I was going to be his best face of fashion, so my two years were more or less guaranteed. This was where the others had gone wrong.

CHAPTER 32

Gino had seen potential in me and gone for it – I was hoping it would always be this way. I wanted to always show I would help him out with anything, taking places of current models, not turning in. I wanted to be one of his most loyal members of staff. I was going to give him 120%. He had looked after me so well and $250k, who earns that?

I couldn't get it out my head. And another $250k, if I did all the fashion shows and modelled clothes as well as my face. I was going to have two years and a million dollars; I would seem like a billionaire if I took that back to Africa, but I wouldn't be going back there until I was famous. The stakes had gone up. If Gino could pay me one million in two years, there was money out there, and I was going to make sure it was going to land in my purse.

The years would go fast and that money would be going in the bank for little work, a bit of pampering as the days of putting my man cap on was now history for two years. I would still have to ensure I always looked good. I didn't want a press man taking a bad photo of me, although I was a natural. But you know girls have that time of the month and so the pimples on your face, including the really big one that captures the whole photo like you have grown another nose. Thank God for makeup. Although I was lucky, my time would come, especially being made up every day.

I could feel it clogging my skin. It wasn't good for saying how nice and smooth and unblemished I was. I don't know what was affecting me, but I had to try and put some kind of a cream base to stop the makeup from messing up my beautiful skin. I would think there would be a price to pay if you were going to participate in this type of work. There could be no compromise in skin damage, especially to my face. That was never going to be an acceptable compromise for makeup that was not compatible with my skin.

There would have to be a foundation cream applied first before they made me up ready for the shows. I would not have my face ruined for a million pounds; I needed these looks to remove money from men's bank accounts and credit accounts. I would even be taking credit cards;

debit cards or charge cards, I wasn't bothered as long as they could pay. It was going to be good in two years of being my own boss.

There would be no early mornings. Most of the parties I would be at were in the evening and through the night. I was never a morning person, so I was going to make sure I worked in a trade that suited my hours and mornings were never going to be an option. It seemed a long time to go, but I also had to collect a telephone diary full of rich people's numbers and give them my card to ensure that they invited me to every occasion.

I would need their birthdays on every name and number, just in case it was getting close to their birthdays, and I hadn't had an invite to the birthday party. I was going to have to mingle to be seen, and I was not going to let any opportunities let me down. There was money to be made; it was the reason I had left Africa.

I needed to ensure regular invites to all parties and fashion shows where I could be seen. There would be no hiding away for me, I needed to be in every magazine and news wherever I was. Publicity was gold to me. I was going to pursue my career as the face of fashion, and I had set my goals out to be what my life's ambition was, to be a socialite. I kept thinking about the money. It bordered on obscene, but I was going to go for the other $250k that was available in extras.

I was in a new place now where I didn't want the money, I had created a need for it now. I could see it building up in my account, I was developing a greed for money, and we hadn't even gotten out of the restaurant yet. It was too much for me to take in up to $500k a year. My dream of becoming a millionaire would be here in two years.

They were going to be the hardest two years ever. If something was available, I was going to take whatever it was. I drew a line at glamour modelling, that was not for me. I was a virgin; no man was even going to see my whole body, although the more men I saw, the worse it got. I wanted a man on me, I had a craving for one, I wanted to feel a man connected to me. My lust for a man was taking over my common sense and inhibitions I had about being a virgin until I was married.

The man of my dreams was going to be the only one to break my life seal and open up my virginity to the world. I had become of age now where it's hard to hold back on nature which was saying I should be producing new species of humans. It would probably be two years before I could even look at having a child, and there was going to be no fatherless child in my life. The man would be here to stay. If he took the leap with me, he'd better be sure he could carry it off.

I was going to ask Gino if I could use the company doctor. I wanted to be on the pill now. I know there are lots of ways of using contraception, but I wanted to take that pill every day. That way I knew it wouldn't go wrong as long as I took them. I wasn't looking for the long haul to be on them, but more of a short fix in case I met a man, and he was too good to be true. I might have to throw my inhibitions out the window and have sex with him.

It was on my mind, but those legs were made for walking and that's what they were going to do. There was never going to be any worktops in a kitchen or a drafty alley somewhere or the back of the car. When I was ready, I would pick the man, then the time and place. It would have to be comfortable so I would enjoy the experience of a man who had been there before. I did not want a virgin boy to be my first experience of sexual penetration.

I was now in an industry of glamour and parties; it was better sooner rather than later. I was taught prevention was better than the cure, and that was right. There are too many children not wanted. I had it in my head that my baby was going to be part of a plan, not a mistake by a man out of control, but conceived properly in a planned-out way. Knowing that the child was wanted and could be cared for by the mother of the child was the way I had been bought up, and I wanted the same for my family.

I was a forward planner, and everything I did had been planned out in detail before I executed the plan. It was the way I had been bought up, as there were no second chances in Africa. It was easy to mess up, and girls did, as there was always a hungry boy not too far away waiting for the opportunity to sow their seeds and take his woman before maturity. They were too young to have babies; they had no experience.

Neither did I, but my head was sitting firmly on top of my shoulders. No man would be coming to knock it off. I would lay awake sometimes in the luxury of Gino's mansion, thinking how nice it would be to be here as my home with a butler and maids plus drivers and security as Gino did. It was small money to him to run his mansion.

I looked at the price of some of the handbags, which would pay my salary for a year on what I was thinking before Gino told me about the salary for the job. I could never tell him what I was thinking as a salary; this would have made me look cheap. My best plan was that I had no friends with me, nobody to share secrets with. I was so glad, as friends can never keep secrets and would have let me down whilst around me. I had no one to be jealous and try to mess up my life.

I was fully in control of my destiny and hadn't done too badly at the moment. Okay, I was on my own, but I had the company of the best man ever, so I was never lonely. I had a TV in my room with all the films to watch as well as the soaps, and I could get lots in English as this was really my first language. I had done well to get here on my own and had grown up some in the last few weeks.

I had changed so fast in my attitude and persona; I had a certain je ne sais quoi about me. It was like I had been here before and here I was doing it again. I was unstoppable in what I did, I was becoming a woman. I was no longer the shy girl trying to put food in her mouth and clothes on her back; I was the woman, the face of fashion. My eyes were firmly on America. That would be my best place to do my fishing when all this fashion modelling was done.

I dreamed about going so many times, but I needed the right connections to get into America. I would now have them with Gino; I was cruising now. It would be nice to stay with Gino for a few years, and I might have a look at designing if I was looking to stay on a bit longer. Possibly 22 would be a good time in my life to go over the pond to America.

CHAPTER 33

I was going to try and spend my time reading up about fashion in the USA and the global industry it represented. It was so rich. This was my ultimate place to do well and make fast bucks. I had a golden opportunity waiting for me, two years of work and I might be on my way. Gino said we would be going to America soon; I couldn't wait to see it all.

I had been daydreaming whilst Gino was circulating around his friends and business colleagues. He was on his way back; I sat up from a slouching position. I had lost my composure. As Gino left, I had slumped into the chair. I sat there like I had been alert all night. They all seemed to be families and couples, all not of the 21st century not the party people I was looking to meet in a few years.

They were all nice but a bit too nice for me, probably a little drab, but drab was safe. There would be no bottles flying around in here tonight. Everyone was just chatting and having a good time. In a way, it was better to be here than at parties. It was safe, but the flip side was that people get drunk at parties and that's where I could pick up a lot of business. In the future, I was looking at the long term, I would just go with the flow and see where it took me. In for a cent in for a dollar.

"Are you ready to go?" Gino said in a soft voice.

"Yes," I replied. "I'm ready for a sleep."

"Right, we will go now. I will phone and get the car bought to the front of the building, and we can go straight away." We got to the door, and we could see there was a scuffle going on outside the door. Three men were fighting and two women, they weren't from here, but Gino said, "Stay here. I will get the drivers to come around the back door. It's not safe to take you out here." *I don't want you in any trouble,* I was thinking to myself. If he only knew my background and how I had to look after myself in Africa.

There was many a big man who went home with black eyes and half my nails in their faces. I was a tiger and had a name. They called me Sabre. If they had heard the stories they wouldn't come near me. Once the nails were out, they were in trouble, I had the punch of a man as well, so black eyes were common for the local men. I had no fear when it came to fighting, there were no holds barred, and I had an insatiable appetite for blood.

If Gino could have known, I would not have been his first choice. I would have to let sleeping dogs lie there, but if we had any problems, I would always be there to fight our way out of a situation. Nobody would ever know, outside of Africa, who they were taking on. Gino escorted me to the back entrance; the guards were there with the car. Standing outside until we had got in, I liked the excitement of it all. I laughed a bit, not sure whether it was a nervous laugh, but I was a woman with no fear, so it wasn't a nervous one but a snigger of what would come if ever I was in a fight. They wouldn't stand a chance. I was a lion of a woman, my routes were born and bred in Africa, and nobody would ever get the best of me.

We were going home, well, home as I knew it now. I would like my own place in the world to own, but for now I was living rent free in Gino's mansion. He was the king, and I was, well I thought, I might have said, the queen, but we were not connected that way. My focus now was on two years of work. If I could get another year out of the face of fashion, on the outside I was calm and collected, but on the inside, I was burning up. The thought of all that money – it was like I had died and gone to heaven.

I was walking on air, dancing my way to the car without Gino seeing me. To him it was a salary. To me it was the world. $250,000 and a possible $250,000 more. It was a dream. Had someone turned the lights on in my head? How could I be so lucky? I was pinching myself all the way to the car. The driver opened the doors, and we were on our way home. In a way it was like man and wife. Everything we did, we did together. It all seemed so close, but I would have been proud to be on his arm any day. He was a babe magnet.

Everywhere we went, the eyes of ladies were on the silky brown eyes of Gino, he was his own face of fashion model. He was so good looking; he was impeccable in his dress sense. I was still in love with him, but I had put that on the back burner. I couldn't afford to make a scandal out of him or break up his marriage. I had my principles, and I was sticking to them. I would not be party to any breakup in the future that Gino might have.

I was so glad just to be in a platonic relationship with him. I could breathe without looking over my shoulder for a press man or his wife being there by surprise. That was not for me. I was clearing a space in my life for a single man, similar looking to Gino but around my age. Just for fun. I had no intentions of getting too serious with him; he would be there for my pleasure. He would have to be good in the bedroom and give me all the attention I deserved. If I wasn't coming, he wouldn't be coming again.

I had my ideal man in my head. I strangely found bald men so attractive, a real turn on, and I certainly would not be fighting for the mirror. It was wash and go for a man like this as long as he never wore a wig which came off in the wind. I was starting to laugh; I had a vision in my head of it flying away in the wind and him chasing after it. If only I could fast forward my mind to be able to see who my boyfriend would actually be, if I even had one.

I was not accepting any freeloader coming into my life and my criteria was no gamblers, no drug taking, no smokers, no smelly men, and no one out of condition with a large belly. I wanted a man who could look after himself. He would have to be the perfect man. I would not carry any freeloader; there would be no man in my life who couldn't look after me. My money was mine and his money was ours; he would have to work hard to keep me.

No short weeks would keep me interested. When you have lived poor, the last thing you want is to slip back into that slippery slope. I made my mind up years ago when searching through dusty dirty clothes, I was never going to go back to those days. It was onward and upwards now. No way would I ever be dragged back there.

CHAPTER 34

I love all my family and friends. They were all real, and I had a feeling after meeting the ex-face of fashion that a lot of people who were going to be coming on to me were going to be false dreamers. I would not even want to recognise people like that; my feet were firmly on the floor. I wasn't floating somewhere in hyperspace; what I said, I would do. There were no frills on me. Just hard facts. I was here, and I would have to be earning my money; it was too little to have the basic $250k. I wanted it all, and nobody was going to stop me getting it.

I was determined and focused on the money. The extra $250k would be a good bonus. I would have to be looking over my shoulder for all the haters. My lips were sealed. Nobody would be proxy to my wages; they were my business and mine only. Being alone made life a lot simpler. I was never trying to hide my bag or my bank statements or cash cheques from my roommate, as there wasn't one, so I slept with both eyes closed in place of one eye open.

I had been used to this, especially with food, if you didn't fancy it or eat it someone would help you out, well, help themselves out to your food. It was acceptable. Nothing was left for later, if you didn't eat it when it was cooked, you had little chance of seeing the food again. It was just the way; nothing was wasted, and we tried to make sure everybody had their share, but the food culprits were always identified by their size.

They would never be catwalk models; they ate everything that was available and did it discreetly. There was no shortage of food here, but I still kept my eye open. *Bad habits die hard,* I thought still looking. I could now buy whatever I wanted. I was just wanting for those zeros to start clocking up in my account. It would take some keeping under control, as I did not want to be squirreling food away in my handbag or under my coat. I had no need, although bad habits made me think. I was telling myself *I'm no longer in Africa it's all free here as much as I can eat.*

That was not a good idea, as I had an insatiable hunger for nice quality food. None was going back to the kitchen. I was the dustbin; I had to make sure the pounds were not going on the bottom side of me to my detriment. I needed to keep this figure. Imagine the press keeping their cameras on the face then standing up and looking like I had gone OTT with food, like I was starving. That's a chance I would have to take. I burned off what I was eating being with Gino; it was unlimited food.

I had to stop the three courses every night, but it was going to be difficult to tell Gino I could not sit down and watch him eating three courses in front of me. I would just have to sit for the main course and stop the starter and sweet, although that would be difficult with my sweet tooth. Sweets were always my favourite; I don't know how I kept my figure.

I was going to do so many things, but I was getting idle and past my remit of being the dream girl, the face of fashion. I didn't want to see someone had put the face of a fat girl on a tabloid one day. I had to keep myself on the right track to keep the perfect figure and ensure I was eating the right food and not the fattening type.

Imagine growing up in Africa and not knowing where your next meal was coming from and what it would be, possibly a bowl of rice. I had not been bought up to eat; I ate like a swallow on the wind. When we could get it, we ate it all. This food now was too much, it was making me greedy. I had been pigging out on it, not thinking about the beautiful figure I have, the fact I was going to ruin it, and that my job would go with it.

From tomorrow, I would be a new girl. Gino had a gym here, so I was on a mission now to use it and trim up. This fabulous body I had been given was not to be abused but worshipped. I was going to make it my temple. There were going to be no more late-night snacks, only meals, nothing in between, and the right meals. I was on a mission to get fitter than a butcher's dog.

Gino must have noticed me a little. There was a tightness in my clothes. I wanted to wear clothes that showed every curve in my body, being in modelling was not an easy business. It was hard work, looking good. I had never witnessed fat; I was always needing to fatten up, not down. It was against the grain to go the other way; it was a constant battle to keep my mouth shut and limit what went in and what came out.

I would have to keep that one under control as well. I didn't want that mouth to get me in trouble. The snack would be off the menu, a main course or a small salad starter and a light main course would be okay, and I would be in the gym for an hour before bed and an hour before work. I could do this if I was focused. Tomorrow was another day. I was going to be a new woman.

I would be in the gym at 7am, there were going to be no midnight snacks anymore. I had got into bad habits; I wasn't going to take them to bed with me anymore. No more squirreling the food away for later. I didn't need later. It wasn't like I was hungry come 12am in the morning. I was just eating out of habit. Since I had been here, I had access to unlimited food but in my nature, living in Africa we would take more food if available and keep it somewhere safe. I had to get away from all these habits. I was no longer in Africa and my earnings were going to be colossal.

Gino had a fashion show set up by his management, and I would now be working from tomorrow. He told me we were going to Centro Congressi Fondazione Cariplo. There was a big fashion show on, but I didn't think I was ready. After cat-walking at the office, where they said "you are more ready than any of the professional models we have," it was my turn to shine, I thought.

This is it. I'm on my way to be a millionaire, I can't wait to be going. I'm going to give my best performance ever, all those days growing up dreaming of being a diva and model were now paying off. All that cat-walking started at seven years old, and I learned myself after watching models catwalk. I had the best catwalk in the business along with my long slender legs.

CHAPTER 35

I was going to be a showstopper. Today my thoughts were just about the money. It's what I had come for, and I was going to look good on that catwalk. It was a big show. Gino had said I would have to be there for 9am to have makeup and hair done as well as a fitting for the clothes I would be wearing on the day. He hadn't said anything about the fashion we were modelling, only that I would be the perfect lady to set the scene and take the catwalk to a different level.

Well, I thought, *I hope it's up a notch and not down one.* Gino said it was a sell out and to be aware of all the photography. It could be blinding in places. I would be the photographers' first choice, as I would be leading them all out. Gino said that was like putting a red rag to a bull, my take on it. All the experienced models, some in their late thirties, being led out by an 18-year-old African black girl – that was going to be something, I thought.

We were nearing the place.

"5 minutes, sir," the driver said to Gino.

"Okay," he replied in a silky Italian voice. He was ready. He had his prodigy next to him and she was going to make him proud of her. As we pulled up in the car, they were all congregating in a circle. I could tell what they were talking about Gino's golden girl. They all seemed to leave the circle as we pulled up; they were waiting to go inside. The doors opened, and they made a rush to get in out the cold. This was going to be a day of fashion to launch the spring collection for one of his biggest fashion designer clothes. It was going to be the biggest opening of spring fashion ever.

We had arrived. The guard got out, opened the doors, and escorted us to the door whilst the driver parked the car. The doors opened.

"Wow." It hit me; the place was something else. It was decorated exquisitely. The catwalks looked so amazing; they were all lit up, waiting for the show to start. I was going to look good there as I walked down. I knew how to draw attention to myself, those days in Africa growing up were not wasted. I would ensure that everybody noticed me and the other models. I wanted that catwalk to be on fire with the show in its full glory.

Gino was excited. He always rubbed his hands together when he was. I had observed things about him in such a short time. He was such a handsome man, every girl's dream, and he was wealthy as well. I had no idea as to his worth, but he was rich, and, when I say rich, he was filthy rich. Everybody regarded him as a fair man, and he could work with the hardest of the women he employed.

There was going to be a catfight here today. I could feel it building up around me. The tension was getting up to hot, and the way it was going, it was starting to boil. It was starting to steam in here with trouble. All eyes were on me. I had done nothing to anyone, but I was happy to be in the vixen's lair, at least I could see who the alfa fox was. I could see her scowling from across the room. *How could she lead us out?* I thought to myself, *she is a pig.*

She should be leading them out of the pigsty. She was a bad one, but I had plenty of experience dealing with people like her. I wasn't going to be intimidated by her. She either kept up with me, or she could sling that hook she was carrying with her and I'm sure it would end off somewhere she wouldn't be expecting. She was the cock of the roost, but I was onto her, and I think she could see it.

She had no style; it seemed she was trying to make herself look good, not the clothes, but she made the clothes look terrible. She had no idea at all what she looked good in. Gino was good like that. He preferred you to model what you could make look good and be the part and look to sell the collection his team had put together. We didn't want it spoiled by a sour face in the corner. She was going to be my understudy now; I was going to be leading the team out and back again for the next catwalk.

We had three to do. It would be a long day, but I had to get it all right to show Gino I was more than capable of looking after fourteen catwalk models. They were putty in my hands, easy to control. I just had one to keep my eye on them. I would have to see how she performed, *old scowler,* I called her to myself. I wasn't bothered about age, but she seemed to depress the rest of the models. There was no fun in anybody. They all seemed tense when I last saw them. I think they just needed someone that could encourage them to enjoy the position of model and to lighten up and make work a happy place. To smile as they turned to look at the audience and not to have a blank look on their face.

I needed to speak to them all in a meeting whilst the makeup was being applied to all the models. Gino had an idea that he wanted the models to look like Amazonian women in their appearance, so there was a bit of work to do before the guests came in. There would always be the dignitaries at the front of the catwalk. I had read these would be the people that wrote about fashion and the show of new collections we were cat-walking today.

I had never walked a proper catwalk, but I had cat-walked our streets and pavements in Nigeria hundreds of times in heels and in flat shoes. Nothing was going to be a problem; all I had to do was keep it all together and make sure nobody was out of synchronisation and everyone walked perfectly whilst on the stage. I was going to have to talk like I knew what I was doing and even make a few stories up about how much modelling I had done throughout Africa. They could not know I was a greenhorn and had never walked a proper catwalk. I had the confidence to do anything if money was involved.

I was going to be the star of the show and Gino would be taking lots of orders for his new collection. I was going to see that the models were wearing the right styles for their height and weight and the clothes suited the looks of the model wearing them. The hair and shoes and makeup had to look stunning. I was going to see I was instrumental to the way they looked and held themselves.

I was effectively taking over. Judging from the catwalk for the press at the office warehouse, there was going to be a different take on this show. I was going to be running it, and if they didn't like it, the models would not be chosen. I would rather do it with ten good models than fifteen bad ones. I had one to sort that out at the moment. I was there. I could not let them know my age, as I would get no respect from anybody. Once we could work as a team, I would be able to control the shows. Somebody might be exiting today if there are any problems. Either she would go with the flow and accept me as the boss or she would have to see the door later.

If she gave me any trouble, she would see the floor. I wasn't going to stand any rubbish today. This was my chance to impress Gino and the buyers from all the stores and outlets. I needed this to be as perfect as we could get it; the press would be here, and it needed to be a hit for them as well.

I couldn't wait to sort it all out; I had to get to know everyone. I walked into the dressing room; the models were all at the bottom of the room in a circle, conspiring, hoping for them to get me out of the business. They saw me come in and it went all quiet and there she was, the ugly duckling, spreading her poison down to all the young models. There were a few scattered around the makeup area. Well, there was no time like the present. I made my way to the bottom of the room.

"Okay," I said. "Can I have your attention, please?" The girls all looked around in dismay. Who the hell was this calling them to attention? Who had given this girl the job as co-ordinator? She was nobody.

I was starting to enjoy my new position. They were not going to try and put me down. I was strong and up there I could see the scowling face of the last face of fashion. She had been constructing some kind of evil concoction. She had bad blood with me, so she had to go.

"Excuse me," I said to her. "Can you leave the building, please? I won't be needing your services today."

She came over to meet me. "Who do you think you are, you silly, stupid girl?" Well, the red flag was out and the bull was on her.

I grabbed her by the arm in an arm lock.

"Let's go. I'm not having any rubbish from you; you were the woman, but now I am and I'm afraid we won't be needing your services for today. Kindly leave the building." I was strong and she picked up on that. She wasn't going to be fighting with me; she could feel the strength of my hands on her arms. I escorted her to the door. She wasn't going to be any trouble, sometimes you have an idea when you are punching above your weight, and she was definitely way above her weight.

She was not going to be taking me on today.

"I'm sorry, love, there is no job for you today. I will be taking your place in leading out the models." Her face turned red with rage; I had to put a bit more pressure on that arm. It was going to end up in a catfight if I let her go. All I wanted to see was her arse out that door.

"Please call the office and sort out a date somewhere in the future," I shouted to her. She was mad, but she knew I meant business. Where was Gino? It was all happening, but I had a clear mandate from Gino to sort out the models and make the show a success, and I wasn't going to let him down.

CHAPTER 36

I just wanted him to leave it all to me, to just relax and leave the day on my young shoulders. I could take the stress of it, as I would take the stress away and make it a professional day. All he had to do was sit back and trust me to get on with it. We had spoken briefly on the way in, and he said he would give me a free reign to do the first catwalk run. I said, "Thank you, and, if it's good, can I be responsible for the other two?"

He looked at me and said, "Let's see if my girl can walk the walk before the talk."

"Yes," I replied. "I can do it; I will do it well."

I have the confidence to do it all. Everybody in makeup would be ready, and all the outfits would be, and it was second nature to the designers now. All I wanted to do was ensure the outfit for the model would be right for her style. I would be sorting it out. I went back into the building and called the models for a meeting.

"Right," I started the conversation. "I now may as well introduce myself for those that haven't met me yet. All I want to know is, are you with me or against me? All against me leave now." They all looked up at that. "I'm now here as the new face of fashion, and I will be instrumental in what you wear on the catwalk. Everything has to be approved by me, as I'm going to put you in something that suites you, and you can feel confident that you are wearing the best things for your body to display the clothes to their most desirable.

"We all have to understand why we are here; we are here to sell clothes and fashion, and we have to look our best to ensure a good promotion of international fashion products. They employ us to do our best job, and I will be leading all the models out on all three events. I want you, on your turn, to smile at the guests and audience, especially the guests, as they will be the buyers and the press and magazines. I'm happy to have you all in my team, but if you let me down, your services will no longer be required.

"It's your job to make sure you have given your best for the company and that, effectively, is what we are here for. To give the company our best, and only your best will be good enough." My thoughts were of Gino and his businesses; I wanted to be instrumental to building his business. We had a fashion show to do, so my focus would be on getting myself and the models ready for the show.

I would make sure that the ones having makeup done now would be fitted out last, and the ones now having makeup would soon be having their fittings done to ensure the right size clothes for the right person. Everyone was going to have to look perfect. My taste was impeccable, and this needed to follow down to the models.

The rooms were starting to buzz with the excitement of the show that was imminent. Now we had only the morning to get ready for the shows at 2pm until 5pm. It was going to be a long day by the time the show finished. Gino seemed to be taking it easy and leaving everything to me. He would not be interfering with my work; I was happy about that. He would be part of the audience and would be out there judging the performance with his associates in the fashion industry.

I would have to make sure it was the best show ever; I had to give him a reason why I got rid of the previous face of fashion. It was an executive decision to remove her from her core position due to causing disruption in the workplace. She would make a good bank model due to her experience, but I was not going to be the one to re-employ her. She was never going to be an envoy for the company. In my short years, I had learned who would be a loyal employee, and she wasn't anywhere in the running for loyalty. She would not be receiving my vote to return to work; it would be only by request from Gino and from his views on her. He was well rid of bad rubbish.

I had effectively done his job and gotten rid of her, I think she knew there was no way back. I had already showed her the door; she would not be knocking again. She had my view on her and had made it clear she would only be needed in an emergency and not on as full-time staff. Wherever she would go, she would spread her poison, but she would not be my enemy. I was in total control of all the show, and I was going to make sure it was a show to remember.

There would be no one inappropriately dressed. Everyone on the catwalk would have been specially trained to give a fabulous show. There could be no excuses about what the models did. They would all have their own job to do, and I would ensure they did it well. I would not accept any refusals to go on the catwalk, even if they were in the first five models. There could be no reason why you would not get on the catwalk and do exactly what Gino was paying you for. Gino was about to see what would happen, and hopefully he would be able to see how organised I was and how I knew how to run a fashion show.

It was only girls, like at school, that wanted organising. If you followed a plan, everything would drop into place. It was just a matter of organisation. I was about to start on the clothes I wanted them to wear; I had already picked a nice little number for myself. It would make an entrance as I stepped on the catwalk. We had to make this day so special. I was going to be instrumental in all the work to get the models onto the catwalk. Today I would be judged by what I had created to make the clothes look so good and ensure the buyers there would be putting in orders for the spring collection.

I would be looking to maximise the money being spent in the fashion industry's time of year. Everyone was having sales, trying to get rid of last year's fashion. It was a new year, 2025, and it would be remembered hopefully for the sales we created with our wonderful fashion show. I had to make sure all the girls had their clothes set out, and I wanted to see every individual model before she went on the catwalk. It was not going to be easy, but I was geared up for this, as though I thought I had been waiting for this my whole life. Well, not my whole life, as I was only just 18 years old, and I needed to lighten up on my organisations.

But I was on it, and I wanted everything to go perfectly. I wanted to see them walk to make sure we had perfect models. Nothing but the best would do. I wanted to make a name for myself in this industry. It was my chosen career, and I was going to make sure it worked for me and Gino. I had the girls all in their clothes. It was a lady's only fashion, we would be doing men soon but weren't not going to mix the days with male models.

I had laid out the clothes for each model and they had put them on; this was my forte, to pick the right clothes and model sizes and shoes with other accessories to go with them. I had been through the accessory box and picked up lots of bits for them to carry or wear. They were going to be the show not steal it; they would all look fabulous. It seemed tweed and silks were the fashion of 2025; Swade was taking over the market, bringing the fashion back to the 70's, but the quality of the Swade and silks were the best.

The way they looked bought in a new era to silks and Swades; they were competing with the tweeds in this show. It seemed to have everything for everybody. There was plenty of choice, and there were no extraverted skirts and dresses. Everything was ready to go and wear, it was thirty minutes away. I had been addressing their catwalking. I sat down, and as they turned around, they would have to smile like I was someone in the front row.

They all seemed to smile, and it looked real, as it was. I had dressed them to look their best and the accessories made them look cool and casual. I could see they were comfortable in what they were wearing and that would be a good sign. The girls were all happy to wear the clothes. If they felt good, they would enjoy showing people how good and comfortable they were to wear.

It was time. I looked through the curtain we were going to walk out of. It was full. I hadn't noticed it filling up so much. The press had set up on the end of the catwalk to get the pictures on the way in and out. You could see all the dignitaries sitting at the front, reading through the magazine for the time slots for the models. We were going to come out twice, as we needed to show the clothes off more to give the buyer a chance to see how good they looked.

I had put all my skills to the test and hopefully excelled myself. It was the moment of truth; it was time to go out. The curtains opened, and we started the show.

CHAPTER 37

I was leading them out. When I stopped, they would stop and turn to the side slightly to show everybody their style and posture to enhance the clothes. We were going and the audience clapped us onto the catwalk. All the girls looked fabulous, and it looked right. We had gone out as a team; the audience was so happy with the models and what they were wearing. I had chosen the right outfits for the right girls; this was fashion as I knew it.

Everyone seemed ecstatically pleased with the models and what they were wearing and carrying as an accessory. I was so happy as I watched as they turned to the audience both ways, smiling away. You could feel that the audience were part of the show, and that's how I wanted it to be. The models were so professional, they were doing exactly what I had shown them to do. Our team would probably be the best in Europe or the world, even. It seemed, in what I had watched on TV and the internet, none of them participated enough with the dignitaries and audience, they were just walking along the catwalk, not paying attention to whom they were walking for.

We had all the buyers here from all the outlets and online sales. I had got them interacting with the audience and the dignitaries and the audience loved it. I had decided to do the walk again, so it was straight back in behind the curtain and out again for a shorter stay on the catwalk, just to refresh the memories of the buyers. We had to make sure it was all going to work, and the buyers would be happy to put in the orders.

I could see Gino at the side of the catwalk, scanning buyers and dignitaries to see who was interested or not showing any signs of giving orders for the new collection. Some of the buyers were standing. They must be really interested to be standing. We went in after our first walk; we had everyone standing and clapping, this was not a normal catwalk. I had pushed them the extra mile and it had paid off; all the models were so happy and proud to be in this event.

I was gaining respect from them; they were all asking where I had learned fashion and how long had I been a catwalk model and if I had been doing it from a young age. They said they were learning a whole new take on catwalk modelling, they never knew it could be so exciting.

"Where did you learn all this?" they were asking. I could see I was going to have to tell an untruth – effectively, a lie.

"I was taught from an early age by my sisters, who were models. They were my mentors. If I put a few of my own creations into the show, I've found a niche that I can pick the right clothes for the right model and make you look your best. I had a really good time growing up, going with my sisters to the fashion shows, watching them, and picking up different ways of walking and showing off the clothes to their best potential."

What a pack of lies I had just told them, but they would believe me, as they had seen the difference with their own eyes. They would not ask me again, but they were there to do their jobs, and I had to get them ready for the second show. At that moment Gino came in.

"Congratulations, what a show. The best I've ever seen. Who's responsible for the organisation?"

"It was Madam Sazzar, she is fabulous," one of the models shouted out to Gino.

"Yes, I can see. The show is buzzing, everybody is congratulating me, but it's you they should be congratulating, Madam Sazzar, and all you models. Your show was off the scale. It was so good, so professional, so I take it you were responsible for all of it, Madam Sazzar."

"Well, not all of it. As you can see, all the girls worked together for the benefit of the company."

"Well, thank you so much. I can't wait to see my new collections; I picked most of the clothes so thank me if there're good. I'm sure you will do a good job on the next line, you all looked fabulous out there. It was the best line-up of models I've ever employed. I want you all to do the same again, as good as the first time."

Madam Sazzar said, "this one is going to be better; I have got it down to an art with the girls now. We are all a team now, and I want to do my best for them, so don't worry about the show, boss; it's all taken care of. We are all going to shine out there." All the girls agreed.

We had a bit of a rapport going on between us. We were all so excited with the show and really wanted to get out there. I had bought happiness to the workplace, everybody was happy. They looked great, and they all made that catwalk their own. They were synchronised together in a natural formation, and everyone was their own person but worked in a team. Everybody was looking after each other, we had become a team, and I was so happy. Even Gino saw the girls were really happy.

We were due to go out again. I looked through the curtains. Everybody was seated, looking forward to the next round. It seemed more press were there than before; it was as if someone had phoned them to get here to this fashion show. We were looking so professional; it was nothing like a normal fashion show. They all looked so with it. The clothes looked fabulous on them; they were going to take the stage.

We walked out into a blaze of flashes from the press photographers. There was so many, nearly three times more. All over the front and sitting on the stairs, you name, it they were everywhere. I took the lead into the blinding lights, but they lifted our spirits so high we felt like we were floating. You could see it in the models as I turned. The audience were clapping so hard and so long. They had never seen a show like it, they erupted with noise from the clapping for us.

This was like winning a gold prize. We were all up there and loving being the centre of attention. Everyone was doing so well on the catwalk; they were all so professional. They just needed someone like me to show them they could do better. We had done our first run of two. I clocked Gino's face coming along the catwalk, he was beaming. He was looking at the amount of press and the interest from the dignitaries and fashion magazines.

CHAPTER 38

He was going to be taking a lot of orders today as so far, the show was booming. Everybody was enjoying the show, even the press man gave me a thumbs up as I took the models off. I had done it, halfway through, and the best was still to come. We had to get in and get changed for the next catwalk. One more session came after, then we would be good to evaluate how well we had done by the orders we were going to receive.

We had to get the second walk over and the grand finale would be the last two walks. We had ten minutes to change, and we were out again. We look amazing with the large hats. It sounded out of place, all wearing hats, but they looked absolutely fabulous. Everybody was standing up, clapping, I had found my niche. Fashion was me all over. I think I was going to be in for a bonus, as it wasn't my job to dress the models; it was my job to be the face of fashion and lead the girls out.

Someone out there in the back was getting paid for nothing. I was thinking we could get rid of her. I didn't need her in my way whilst I was working. I was assuming that nobody had dressed them properly; I had an eye for putting things together. I would have some feedback at the end of the show. I had never seen so many bare women; it seemed they were not shy in showing off their nude bodies. They all had stunningly beautiful figures, so it was just women and the regular men that bought the clothes. Nobody paid attention to anybody, everyone just got on with their job.

We were getting ready for the last run; we had some clothes that were effectively not fashion for this year but were really different. I had mixed and half matched them, but I was good at making different clothes look good. They were not matched, but they all looked so different. I was stretching my talents for matching the models to the clothes. I was going to excel. If the time had been better, I could have really pushed the boat out, but I was hurried, and I had to make some snap decisions.

I wasn't trying to sell last year's fashion, but if I could do my magic on the clothes we had, I'm sure I might just scrape through. We were good to go, all lined up to go through the curtain onto the catwalk. As I walked out, the applause was rapturous. All the people were standing up in awe of the way we all looked. I had dressed them casually, but they looked magnificent. I wasn't sure, but they loved it. The finale was a major hit. The cameramen were going crazy to get the best photos for their paper or magazines.

All the models could feel the difference and had never had such a rapturous applause. They were all standing as we passed by again. This was going to be it. We would come back out, but for now we were on our way back in. We would come back for one more run, all turn at the same time to the audience, and turn and go back in. We came out. We could see Gino's staff were inundated with enquiries; they were queuing to put their orders in.

There was a rapturous clapping as we were going back in. Thank the lord for that. I was so nervous, though I had not shown any signs of it, deep down I was bricking myself. We got back. I had been blinded by the flashlights and I was seeing double, but I was so glad I was in and finished. All I had to do was get changed. Gino stuck his head in give me the thumbs up as we were behind the screens getting changed.

It had gone well. The girls had been so professional, and they couldn't thank me enough. I had changed them from catwalk models to catwalk stars in one afternoon. I was everybody's friend; it was strange, I thought to myself, how fickle life is. In a few hours, I had gone from their enemy to a friend. This was all caused by the bitching from the ex-face of fashion. Where was she now? I thought. I hope she was sitting in the back somewhere, watching. She would have never believed it was just me that had put it all together.

There was no intervention from anybody but me. I was going to start making a name for myself by changing the concept that was sixties fashion. There had to be more interaction with the buyers, the press, and the paying audience. They needed to see a real fashion show, one of the twenty first century, so people could appreciate the time we had put in. Without them, it just didn't work.

It was old and boring. I hope I had put another perspective on fashion; it would never be the same again. I hadn't revealed all of my ideas; I had to have some ammunition to fire in the next shows. I had it in my head to produce more than the next fashion but a fabulous show to attend, invited or not. Fashion needed to remain exclusive but not impossible to attend shows and see fashion at its best before seeing it in the shops. It would create a whole new way of people enjoying fashion and it would be a show to remember. People could look out for what they liked when it was available in the shops.

I looked out of the curtain; there was a queue to put names down to receive a catalogue, there was a queue for people waiting to reserve a place in the orders, the press was packing up, and Gino was mulling around the hall. He was socialising with the dignitaries as they were all connected, it was busy. It would be a while. I was hungry and needed something to stop me collapsing on to the floor. Just a snack would be alright.

I was that busy with my nose outside the curtain that I was missing the buffet Gino had laid on. I soon got over to the other side of the room. I was on it. I had lots of food on my plate, but I was not thinking straight, as this is how I was putting on weight. I wouldn't look good with cellulite all over my legs and bottom. I had to start limiting what my stomach was telling me and limit the food I was eating. When I was in Africa, that was more like it; I was conscious about my figure.

I had to be the best. I couldn't look anything else but the best. We lived in a world where nothing mattered anymore, but I was probably going to be one of the most famous models in the world and cellulite was not acceptable to me. I needed to be the perfect person. We had moved away from perfect but a pretty woman with a great figure is always going to be a head turner, and that was me all over. If I wasn't turning heads, what good would I be as a model?

I wanted people to recognise me. I was out there, and I wanted the whole world to know me. I wasn't vain, but I wanted the fame as I know I could take it to the next level, and I had to make sure I would always be the girl to be invited everywhere.

CHAPTER 39

It was my turn to shine, and I was not going to accept any less. I would always be striving to be the best; nobody would be able to knock me off my perch. I would be looking over my shoulder for all the haters, but I could handle anything they threw at me. I wasn't scared to take any of them on. I sat on my own to get my thoughts sorted out, I was on it. I wanted the next fashion show to include me from the beginning.

Next time, instead of my fire rescuing I had just taken part in, I needed the next to be more relaxed and with little fuss. If I knew what everybody was wearing, I could work around it and at least make everything flawless. I needed the time to make the show perfect; I would talk to Gino on the way home and see what he said.

It was a routine that he had probably gotten into, and it would always fall into someone's lap to organise. This is why the previous shows were just average; I had to make the girls go to the next level. Nothing else would do if it wasn't perfect. If I was anything, I was a perfectionist. My standards were right up there at the top, and we were not going to scrape along like a bottom-feeder ocean fish – all that would be doing is eating rubbish something else left behind.

The last face of fashion had left. Now that was behind us, she would not be returning, so the show was all mine now, for good or for bad. I was going to make damn sure it was for good; no ex-employees would be coming back. I was someone that always looked forward. What was gone stays gone in my book. I was having no bitching going off between the girls, they were on my team now, and we would work in unison together.

It was all for Gino's ears on the way home, so I was geared up to tell him where I wanted to go with it all. I was thinking there would have to be more organisation, especially at the big shows like today, these needed more time to organise. I wasn't sure what was in Gino's head, whether or not he wasn't thinking about how it was all going to go, but I also thought he was testing my skills. What if it had all gone horribly wrong and we all looked like new recruits in place of the professionals we were?

That wouldn't have been good for the company, and Gino wouldn't have been the person he is now. I'm sure he would have gotten rid of me; I was counting my blessings as he seemed so happy. I was just hoping I had covered everything and not left anything out that I should have included. Oh well, we were all getting ready to go home now. I must say I was ready to go as well; it had been a really busy day. I must say I had enjoyed it to the max. All the girls came to me and said goodnight, they all looked so happy.

I was thinking to myself, *I hope their smiles and politeness are real,* I would like to think I had bought them some good ideas in. They had all enjoyed their time at work today, after all those cameras and applause had not stopped, so hopefully I had done my job and made some orders today for Gino. I could see him talking to his clerical staff who were taking orders.

They were about finished, and I could see them packing away as well, so that was my indication to get ready to leave. I was hoping for a really nice healthy dinner when we got back to the mansion. I was ready for any criticisms Gino had for me on the way home. I saw one of the staff bring some flowers and give them to Gino. He was going to probably put them up in the house. Well, at least I would be able to find out if he was happy with the way things had gone.

He was smiling as I looked over. I thought *well, I must have done something right*. I started to walk over, and he came up to me and gave me the flowers.

"These are for you, Madam Sazzar, for pulling of the best show we have ever had. Where are you coming from?" he said.

I replied, "Africa."

Gino laughed. "No, my dear I meant how did you learn all the moves? The catwalk was fabulous. Everybody was talking about the show, how wonderful and professional it was, and they absolutely loved the clothes.

"Who picked them out and all the accessories they were holding and wearing? Where did it all come from?"

"Well, from my head," I replied.

"Well," Gino said, "You are an amazing woman. It was the best day ever meeting you on that plane. I want you to choreograph all of my shows now with your team wherever we go. You will be in charge of everything, I will see that, as my income increases, so will yours. You have an unbelievable talent, and I want to see I keep you with me."

"That's not a problem," Madam Sazzar said. "I'm loyal to one person and that's you. I met you and you put your faith in me; I was never going to let you down."

Gino replied, "Well, we are taking record orders; every dignitary here has placed an order for our spring collection. We are sold out until the summer collection; we will be struggling to keep up with our orders, but I'm sure with some overtime for the employees we will be on target for our best year to date, and it's all because of you. This will be in all the magazines and on TV channels."

"TV?" Madam Sazzar replied.

"Yes, they were at the rear. Their cameras are digital now and no longer the size they used to be, so the whole show will be going worldwide. Your family will be able to see it in Africa as well.

"The images will be really good, as the TV cameras were triangulated to get shots from every angle."

It's going to look so good on TV, I thought to myself. What if my family see me here? How will I explain myself to them that I abandoned them to pursue my career? That doesn't go down well in Africa. We are supposed to look after our family, but I could send some money back to support them in their needs. That was the answer. When I got paid, they would get paid, too, as they are my family and I wanted to see them live a good life. Whatever Gino gave me, I would send some to them.

The drivers turned up. It was time to make our way back home. Italy had become my second home, and I was happy to be here. I had effectively been locked away in the mansion except for the benefit of going to places with Gino, but I would be getting out to work now and not sitting around the mansion getting fat. I needed to be active. I was going to be in the gym every day to keep myself in perfect shape. It was a trudge to keep myself in good condition, but I could not afford to go up a size. Too much was riding on this beautiful figure of mine.

I had to keep away from all the nice things in life to eat and have just a small treat sometimes. We were in the limousine going home and Gino opened the bag; he had a bottle of champagne.

"Here we are," he said. "Let's toast to a bright future for you, Madam Sazzar." Gino put the glass in my hand and filled it to the top. How was I going to be able to drink it? I thought.

"Bottoms up," he said. I wasn't even sure what he meant by that, but, as he put the glass to his mouth, I could see the bottom of the glass.

This is what he meant. He wanted me to drink mine like he was drinking his, "bottoms up." I raised my glass.

There was nothing here to be scared about as I drank the champagne. Gino filled my glass. It was a thirty-minute journey, so I had plenty of time to have a drink. I had never drunk much alcohol, only a few times mainly at weddings. I was feeling tipsy already, I wouldn't be able to take the next glass. I wasn't used to drinking champagne, but the bubbles excited my nose as I drank it. I was getting to like it so much, but I could feel my head swimming.

I was going to pass out, I had only had two glasses. What a light weight I was. I could see Gino from the corner of my eyes, the car was spinning around along with everything else. Had I been drugged? I asked myself. How could it be my head was swimming around it was only fizzy pop I had been drinking?

We got to the house; the driver opened the door, and I fell out onto the drive. The driver just managed to catch me.

"Can I help you in, Madam?" he said. Well, I wasn't sure what he said, I was drunk, but how could I be drunk on two glasses of fizzy lemonade? I'm sure somebody had drugged me. I could hear Gino he was saying to somebody, "Are you alright? Can I give you a hand up?"

Someone had fallen over. He was a kind man.

"Madam Sazzar, are you alright?" I thought *yes, I'm alright.* I was looking around to see who needed help. The whole world was spinning around. I couldn't seem to focus on anything, I could see the shadow of a man who looked a bit like Gino.

All I could hear was, "Madam Sazzar, are you alright?" Who was that? How did he know my name? This was ridiculous. Why couldn't I stand up? There was something wrong; the drive must be slippery. *If I can hold the door, I might be able to get up. The world keeps spinning. What's the matter with everybody? Why are they around me?* I wished they would go and help someone that needed help. There was nothing wrong with me. "Go away and help her over there," she said.

The driver, I heard him, he said, "she is off her trolley, sir." What did he mean by trolley? I came in a car.

CHAPTER 40

Gino was laughing a bit; somebody must have made a funny joke up. I never heard him laugh much, but it was definitely him. I wanted to get up so I could have a laugh too, but for some strange reason I couldn't stand on my legs to get up. Someone was holding me down. I was struggling to get up, I felt like I was glued to the floor. I felt somebody picking me up.

"Get off," I heard myself saying. I was being carried towards the house.

I couldn't focus on anything in front of me; the people's faces seemed blurred. Had I been in an accident? Were these medics taking me into the hospital? It didn't look like a hospital; I couldn't keep my eyes open. I was drifting in and out of consciousness. Where was my phone?

"Can anybody see my phone?" I felt it go into my hand. Someone had found it and had given it to me. I needed it to phone the hospital, and I needed to know why my head was spinning. Was I at the end of my life? It felt like it.

I had been here before. I could see the chandeliers and the large staircase. I saw the maid. Had she been getting the beds ready? What was she doing? It was only dinner time. I was feeling quite ill, I was struggling to open my eyes, but I could see the apron of a woman. What was she doing here? The next thing my head thumped against something hard. I was about to go out.

I woke up with a banging head. I ran to the bathroom; I felt like throwing up. As I was bending down, my head hurt on the top. Had I fallen over? I had a large bump swelling on my head. Had I fallen over during my illness last night? I don't know still why I was so ill, whatever it was, I wasn't well. I made my way down for breakfast. I was hungry – probably that's why I felt poorly this morning.

I had been trying to be sick but only releasing bile. I was poorly, I'm not sure if it was because I didn't eat much. I couldn't think or remember falling. I was going to ask Gino at breakfast what happened. I was curious how I got this lump on my head. I must have fallen out of the car and bumped my head. I walked into the dining room. Gino got up as usual as the gentleman he is.

"How are you, Madam Sazzar?"

"Well, I was going to ask you a question, if you don't mind," I replied.

"Can you tell me if I fell out of the car last night?"

"Well," Gino said, "you only had two glasses of champagne, and you were out of it, but it was strong."

"We don't tend to drink a lot of alcohol in Africa."

"Well, it was a celebration. You were so professional, and we took the biggest order we have ever taken. It was all down to you and the fabulous show you put on. It was off the scale on the catwalk. We had to carry you up the stairs. You were unconscious; it must have knocked you out. I got the maid to put you in bed."

"So, you never dropped me then."

"No, Madam Sazzar, you're too valuable to be dropping. I made sure you were safe all the way to your bedroom."

"Oh, thank you," I said.

"Well, sit down," Gino said. "let's have some breakfast. I bet you're as hungry as me."

"Yes, I am," I said. "I could eat for Africa."

"Well, let's eat for Italy today," Gino said. The food was so welcome, the maid bought some croissants out.

"Here you are, sir, just as you ordered."

I looked up, and she gave me a look like I was dirt under her feet.

She was shying away; she had traitor running through her like a name through a stick of seaside rock. She was the one who threw me down on the bed. I remembered a crack of noise as I hit the headboard. That bitch was instrumental in the bump on my head; I had no real proof as I was half out of it, drunk. I would not be drinking again; I don't like it when I'm not in control of my senses.

I was thinking it was her that put that lump on my head. She looked guilty, and she wouldn't look me in the face. I had her card marked. I wished I could only have some proof. My head was throbbing from the alcohol and the bump was sore at the back of my head. There would be no more opportunities like that again, she had fired her first and last bullet. It was going to be my turn, but I needed some kind of evidence. I now knew it was her, and I was going to take her to task the very first time she stepped out of line.

I was full, I couldn't eat anymore. I had been selective and stayed away from anything that would put weight on me. This body was now my temple more than ever now, and I was going to look after it and keep as fit as a butcher's dog. They are never fat; I was not going to be either. I could see the maid had a scowling face, I've seen too many of them in my short years. She was never going to be anywhere more than she was now, but I think she had her eyes on the boss.

I had come in and burst her bubble. If she only knew I was no threat to her, she might have treated me differently, but it was going to be outright war now. She had attacked me when I couldn't fight back. She was never going to get that chance again. Her fighting days would soon be over when I had a hold of her. She had woken a sleeping lion, and she was going to pay for the treachery she had shown last night.

I was vulnerable and she took advantage of my condition, I heard someone swearing in the bedroom last night. It could only have been her; she wouldn't have gone off shift until nine pm and we left at seven pm, so I was in the bedroom possibly around eight pm. She had time to work her poison, and she made sure I was going to pay the price for my intrusion into her life. She was obviously trying to truss Gino up so she would be his.

I think he would have looked twice at her before. He was not stepping out of line for her; she wasn't the best. Her problem was that she had been outclassed by me; I was miles in front of her, and she knew it. She was just a maid wanting to go up the ladder fast, straight to the top, by enticing him into the bedroom. Merely lying on her back in the bedroom was not going to be the long-term strategy for Gino and her. She thought it might be. She had worked for him for five years, so if nothing had happened in five years, nothing was going to.

I had my eyes focused on the competition, but there was no competition, only a maid with a dream who had turned vicious in the presence of beauty. She was not going to win this war. It was already won; I was not in a race to win anything. I was happy with my status, and nobody was going to be instrumental in ruining our relationship. Gino was up there. She was trying to go to the next level, but I had my head on my shoulders and no one would be knocking it off. I had my feet firmly on the ground.

CHAPTER 41

I now knew exactly where I would be going; I was no longer dependant on anyone now. Gino had given me total control of the fashion shows, looking after all the catwalk models and ensuring they looked the best in the latest fashion. I wanted to also be more instrumental in fashion design, but I would probably have to put it all on the back burner for now.

I needed to have more time doing what I was paid for, being the face of fashion. It was my job to lead out the models, and it was their job to follow my instructions. I seemed like a taskmaster but underneath I was hard inside with a soft exterior that made me look approachable and kind. That was the impression I wanted to promote.

I was a good bad person, and they didn't want to meet the bad side of me; it would be awful for them. They would be thinking they were taking on a lamb, but they would be taking on the tiger stalking the lamb. I had full control of my senses, and I had my eye on everybody.

Nobody would be doing less than the job they were paid to do; it all had to be above board to me.

I had been bought up to respect my family, friends, and bosses and to keep my enemies close but my friends closer, as sometimes your friends are your worst enemies, waiting for the right opportunity to stab you in the back. I was having none of this. I was out there watching out for everyone that was potential trouble. If I found it, I could nip it in the bud before the poison was out.

I wanted to be close to all the models but not so close I could not see what was going off. I had had so much experience growing up. Africa was the best place in the world to grow up, you learned so much about life. There was never a dull moment, you never had time for dull moments. It was bad enough having to be streetwise.

I had some sorting out to do with the maid. She had burned every bridge she had, and she was now on my blacklist. If you knew me it was not a good place to be. She would soon be paying the price for her treachery. I was incapacitated by the drink of champagne, but she was due to be incapacitated, and it would not be drink that was the driver to her misdemeanour.

She was an open target for a tyrant to take her revenge. She was unaware that I had just found a conversation on my phone which had recorded when I was incapacitated. She had been calling me bad names. She said, "sleep well you fucking bitch," as she slung me against the headboard. I could hear my head hitting it as I went down. She was dangerous, but she had more than met her match.

I would serve my revenge cold, just like I got, but she would not be fairing so well. I had to make sure the plan was going to work without incriminating myself. I had seen things go wrong in Africa with revenge, but I had to keep a clean slate as she was the maid, and Gino wouldn't approve of what I wanted to do. The lump on my head didn't seem to be going down too fast. It was a real vicious attack, and it was on track to happen to her.

Her cards were marked, and I would be calling them in for retribution. I had to clear my mind of her and put on a smile for her every time she saw me so she would think that sleeping dogs were lying. I wanted her to think that way so she would never suspect me; it would be all over in a flash.

I knew America was on the books, and Gino was going to take me there. I was ready to go there. I had heard so much about it, it was the place to go, and it was where I wanted to spend a lot of my life. Socialising amongst the rich and famous of Hollywood, New York, and Florida sounded really good to me. I could do some good business there; I was hoping to clean up over there.

There was a golden opportunity to do well over there, it was the land of opportunity. It was virtually in my grasp, and I was frothing at the mouth to get it all. I would be the biggest socialite America had seen in a hundred years, when the stars of film were big and famous. I wanted to work my charm; I had realised the opportunities were out there, and I would have to milk it for what it was.

I wanted it all now whilst I was young, I didn't want to have grown old. Everything was there for the taking, and I was going to ensure I took more than my fair share. I was taught opportunity only comes once so take it whilst it's there. I was desperate to get to America, I would have to see if I could give Gino a push to get me on the way.

We had the spring collection to catwalk in Paris, New York, and London. London would be the last stop before the summer clothes were released. I was excited to see what was going to be the new fashion. I was always working three months ahead of myself; I had to get some of the fashion shows away. London and Paris were looming, and I would have to be ready for New York and Los Angeles.

It wasn't far away that Gino would be showcasing another fashion for America. Some of the garments would be there, but we were going there to ensure everything would go well. We had a few days at home, well, okay at my lodgings, free, of course. I was doing well at the moment, free lodging and board, all food included. Well, it couldn't get much better than this, my boat had come in and I was out there cruising.

All I had to do is keep my head down and do my job. I was getting used to it all, I was a fast learner. The bitch had gone. I got one to still sort but that was not going to affect my work and personal life. She was marked and standing in her shoes was not a good place to be. Every dog had its day and hers would not escape her.

We were going to LA, America; I was so excited, I couldn't wait to go. I went to bed thinking about my dream. This was where it was all going to happen, nothing was going to stop me. I had dreamed about America as long as I could remember. I thought about it every day right down to seeing the northern lights as we travelled across. I had so much going off in my head. I was young, so my brain was like a sponge taking everything in as I saw it or heard it.

I was not one for letting too much out of myself. I was very secure when it came to releasing any information. I was waiting for a phone call from my siblings, as they always watched the fashion shows. I was wondering if they had seen the Milan fashion show, but I knew they watched the New York and LA fashion shows. I wanted them to see me leading the catwalk. It was going to be bigger than Milan, but Paris was the one everyone set their benchmark to.

It was the most prestigious. The thought of going to these places set me on fire. I couldn't wait; how could I have been so lucky as to meet Gino? I would never have met him if I hadn't blagged my way into first class. It was so good being there. I would have to keep my eyes on Gino – I knew what he was like now. After chatting to me, he wasn't flirting, but I felt his eyes on me as we spoke.

I was sending him the signals, and he had picked up the message. I had clearly manipulated him into semi-consciousness, and he had come into the trap. All I had to do was reel him in. It wasn't that simple with Gino; he was there for something else. He had seen something in me he wanted. I know it was about how much money I could make him as a perfect uplift, a replacement for my predecessor.

He had engineered the whole thing, and I was of the thinking that I was the clever one, but he had played his hand and won. I was defeated by a superior adversary I never knew. Although I would be happy with anything he was offering, apart from intimacy. That was definitely off the menu. I met him going into the dining room, I was so hungry I could have eaten it all.

The food was unbelievable. It seemed nothing was any trouble; we lived like kings. If only my family was here. I could feed them all with the amount of food that was here, it was well overloaded. If I overstayed my welcome, I would turn into a bouncing baby girl. I couldn't afford to lose my figure. It was the way to the millions, and it's what I had come for. Gino was well relaxed, being served by the butler; he was up there somewhere floating in the clouds.

To me, he was living a king's life, he had it all. This place was like a palace and the food was to die for. It was enough to make anybody put on three dress sizes in a month. I thought about having my jaw wired up so I could only take liquids, but I thought I might be able to handle it. If I have one course and leave the appetizer, the starter, the sorbet, the main course, and the sweet.

CHAPTER 42

Just talking about it made me put on weight. It was as if my stomach had blown up with an expectation of a large amount of food about to come down. Well, it could forget that. It wasn't happening. I was going to have to half starve myself, it wasn't my body that needed it. The culprit was my greedy eyes that could see it and sent a clear message to my brain that food was on the way.

I needed to put a pair of beer goggles on to stop it looking at what was going to ruin my career. It's those mincers that were going to look at me in the mirror. I had to take control of everything. I could do just having breakfast and nothing more. It was hard to be in an industry where fashion was based on the model. I was going to have the perfect body I've always had; I had never been overweight. Nothing wrong with that, a lot of men like the larger woman, and we had some on our catwalk.

We had to cater for all tastes. There would be no skeletons walking on my catwalk, everything was geared up for the fashionable lady, and they're the ones out there looking good. It seemed all the sizes for women were bigger in the shops, but that was not in my mind. I had been the same size since I reached it. I had no reason to make the size change; it was my look, and I wanted to keep it.

I wasn't going to lose this body; it was a magnet to men, and I wanted to ensure an easy passage into the world of wealth. A good, fit, good-looking woman – it was like shelling peas when it came to men. I had a way of attracting them. I was so ready for the flight to America. Just to think, Gino had paid for two first-class return tickets. I wouldn't like to have picked up that fare, but I heard in Nigeria that companies that travel regularly get better rates. They couldn't possibly get it cheaper than I did, but that was a one-off.

The food was, as usual, fabulous. I had the veal, which was thin cut, and the veg was so nice: broccoli, asparagus, green beans, and fried mushrooms. It was so good I was about to ask for it again, kicking myself about the calories in it. Modelling was all about counting calories. I had been selected by Gino for being the person I was, and I was not changing to suit the social media that we should be who we are regardless of size.

My view was you have to work hard at something if you want it to be something. I learned nothing comes out of nothing, so I was going to make myself into a somebody, and I was well on the way. One good meal was enough for me, and I wasn't feeling it anymore. I just had to focus on other things when I was hungry.

Two days to chill out, and it was America; it was going to be a long wait two days when I was desperate to go. I was going to use the pool and do some swimming to relax my mind and tone my body so I was ready to go. Gino had told me to take any clothes out of the fashion show we had just cat-walked. I had my eye on a few garments, but I wanted to make some alterations to them; they were not quite what I wanted. I could re-sew them make some changes, and they would be good.

It would keep me busy for now until the flight. Hopefully, if the driver could take me to the office warehouse, I could select the ones I wanted in the morning. Gino had told me to help myself, so I had my mandate to sort out my wardrobe for the trip. I had to get working to get them ready, I needed them; I was wearing the same clothes every day. I wanted to look dynamic for Gino; he was going to be my chaperone and take me any where I wanted to go for dinner or a drink.

He was so good. What a man to have in your life – nothing was too much trouble. It's amazing: when you're busy, time always goes fast. The travel day was nearly on us; I had sorted all my clothes. I had finished all the alterations. I hoped Gino liked the changes I had made to his new collection. He might one day employ me as a fashion designer, I was right up there with fashion, and I wanted to be instrumental with the collections: summer, autumn, and winter.

Fashion weeks would be soon, only around the corner. Maybe in between I could design a new collection. I had good fashion sense, and I could also do the way-out garments, so I had diversity in my mind and could create fashion that was different from others. I had found that fashion had taken a downturn in its innovation of clothes. They were usually unwearable or too mundane so nobody wanted to wear them. Same old same old.

We had to use the company to set all the new fashion trends. It would never be the same again if I was in control of what was designed and worn by people all over the world. I wanted to be more than the face of fashion; I wanted to be global fashion, taking everything to the next level. I would not be satisfied until I was indispensable and Gino was making a place for me as a director of fashion.

The bar had now been reset at the highest level, and I had faith in myself to get to the top. Nothing would stop my march to the top. I was on my way, I just needed Gino to open the door and give me the opportunity to show my skills. I had his trust. All I was looking for was a piece of the action, a full directorship with shares in International Fashion.

It was all in my head, but I was going to make it a reality. It was just a matter of timing. It was in my mind to negotiate when I was in a stronger position. If it worked, I would be an instant millionaire. and Gino would have the best fashion in the world. I was already opening doors, and I was engineering myself into a better position. I sounded like a poison chalice, but I was giving good value for money. If the brands I designed took off and went viral on the internet, Gino would be cruising.

Time would tell, I was thinking to myself. I would have to wait until I was indispensable and then play the five-card trick. I had to look after my own destiny, and, as long as Gino's profits were moving up, I would be worth the investment. For now, I was looking forward to my travel and the experience of America. This was going to be my home; I would buy my way in if I could prove my worth, but I would probably be accepted as an asset.

CHAPTER 43

Gino called up. It was today. We were going. I had so much on my mind I had lost sense of time. The drivers were ready to take us to the airport; I was a bit rushed, and I came out into the hallway still trying to put my stiletto heels on. I heard the door shut behind me; I had left my key inside, so if I had forgotten anything it would have to stay.

I had my fabulous bag Gino had given me; I had no money. Gino had ordered me a charge card and debit card, but they hadn't arrived. Shame, I was going to be Gino's guest again; it was his turn to pay. Laugh out loud. That would be a good idea for money saving, well, no I wouldn't do it. I would love to buy dinner out for us, but Gino wouldn't accept it as he said everything business was on the slate. He wasn't paying out of personal monies; he said that would be like paying taxes twice. It was never going to happen.

I was happy with my position and the salary; it would be nice if my thoughts came to fruition, but that was in the future, not to distract, I thought. We were at the airport. It was all VIP. Gino just got out as the driver opened the door; I got out the other side when the other driver opened my door. Whatever happened to ladies first? Well, I suppose Gino was the bill payer, so I would have to take my place. He was the wage payer for his staff, so he deserved the curtesy of being let out first. It made sense as he sat behind the driver in the passenger seat.

We went through a different passport control; the people actually knew him. They greeted him with respect and kindness. They knew who he was, and we went through without a queue. I would suppose he had earned the right to go through without the hassle of a normal person; he had moved up to the top. He wasn't a normal person, but he was a gentleman. We was well-respected everywhere. No one had a bad word to say about him; we were escorted onto the plane first class.

I was becoming used to this now. Well, only one flight, but you realise you don't want to travel any other class. Only the best will do now. I had become the prodigy for Gino; he was going to teach me all the things he knew about fashion. I was a sponge; I wanted to learn everything. I would be in the right place to learn with Gino and in America, my dream home.

We got settled in for a seven-hour flight. I had everything I needed in my new bag. I looked a million dollars.

Gino leaned across, "I was wondering if they were some of the clothes out of our spring collection."

"Well," Gino said, "I never saw them looking as good as that. I couldn't take my eyes off you. I couldn't say anything in front of the drivers, you look remarkable. So beautiful. I'm proud to be with you, I'm going to enjoy this break."

"Can I ask if you have cannibalised any others of the spring collection?"

Madam Sazzar said "er, I'm afraid so, but I think you will be pleased with the job I've done on them."

"Well, if its anything like what you're wearing now, you're going to be putting my designers out of work."

"Oh, I wouldn't want to do that," I replied.

"I'm sure it was just a bit of tailoring you did. It does look fabulous on you. Maybe we could adopt this revamp to the designed spring collection."

Madam Sazzar had been quiet listening; I had been told it was always better to listen than talk unless you had something good to talk about. I had been thinking about what Gino said about the designer. I was going to make sure that collection had a major refurb. It was good, but not good enough for me; I wanted it to be like no other. This I could sort out when we were back. I was going to make it all look amazing.

I think I would be taking over the designs in the near future, all the collections would be my designs. I could get rid of the best, take their salaries, and add them to mine. If Gino wanted the best, I was going to give it to him. He had been thinking about how I had turned the garment completely around and done it all myself, the cutting, the stitching, everything was carried out by me.

He was aware of my other skills, and he was thinking about his next move. I could hear it all whirring about in his head. I was beginning to get to know him, and I was going to show him what a valuable asset I was to the company. I excused myself. I could feel his and every other man on the planes' eyes burning through me. I knew how to make a man look, even Gino, in his empire of women workers, was on me.

I wouldn't go the extra mile with Gino; he was my boss, but it didn't deter me from bringing a bit of excitement into his life as he was the man and he knew fashion and women. It would not look good, the man of international fashion dating his worker, the eighteen-year-old face of fashion. If he couldn't control himself, I would do it for him. Probably staying a virgin for a few years wouldn't be a bad thing.

It would keep the men away; what you have never had you have never missed. If I had been involved with a man, I would have been looking to jump into bed. At the moment, I was ready to jump in bed and get some sleep. There would be no late night for me, no babies to look after that would spoil everything I had planned. Babies were for when I was thirty years old. I wasn't going to leave it too long as I didn't want to be an older mother. Thirty was a good age. I could do and see a lot in those years, and I would be more ready to settle down.

For now, I had all the attention I required. I wouldn't be filling my diary here. Gino clearly had his eyes on me; I wasn't uncomfortable with that, but his eyes had suddenly become hungry. I could tell this: when a man has hungry eyes, it would be a dangerous place to be because a lot of men want to control you. I was a tiger. No man was ever going to control me, more like me controlling him.

If he didn't like it, the shop would be closed for close contact. I had made my mind up that that love thing could destroy my career, so I was not going to bother. When I had a friend to go clubbing with, why would I need a man? Until I was ready, I was going to milk this industry to the max. I would, of course, give good value for money, and my goal was to increase the wealth of Gino's company so I could be his top woman forever.

I had no plans to leave Gino. He was a good boss and so good-looking and such a sociable person. I had it all with him, I was just hoping he would never turn into a bad boss. It was not in his genes; I sat there looking at all the seats and who was sitting on them. This was the life. I had everything covered.

CHAPTER 44

I couldn't wait; we would be in during the night. I was hoping it was nearly dawn so I could see the northern lights; it was one of the things to knock off my bucket list. Just as I was thinking about it, Gino moved away from the window.

"There you are, look out there." As sure as eggs are eggs, there they were, absolutely fabulous. I had never ever seen lights like that before; the colours were totally unbelievable and so beautiful.

I had never seen anything like it in my life; I stared out the window until we had passed them. I was like a child, but I was mesmerised by the beauty of them. Gino had seen them all before lots of times. He was just watching something on his laptop. The landing was a bit rough due to cross winds, but I had had a chilled-out flight. It was difficult to work with Gino being there. He knew how I worked, and I think he would have taken my diary off me.

There would be plenty of flights in the future to fill my diary up. I was committed for two years, so I would have to keep my head down until I had finished my time with International Fashion. Although I was hoping a directorship was going to be in the making in the future, if I could make myself indispensable. I had been to the bathroom three times and cat-walked the plane just to draw a bit of attention to myself, but we were on the ground, and we were about to exit the plane.

It was nice to be the first off the plane; I could see all the people in the lower classes waiting. I felt very important coming off early, but I deserved it as I had put the work in to get here. Gino was the gentleman, as usual, letting me go first and carrying my bag. It had quite a lot of things in it, including the kitchen sink. I wasn't a light traveller; I had so much to take with me. I needed a lot more room in my cases.

A porter came, took my bag off Gino, and escorted us to passport control. He was obviously known to everybody; he was treated as a celebrity. How rich was this man that he should be shown this much respect? I loved the attention of people looking at us exiting the staircase and the porter carrying my bag. It would have been me carrying someone's bag two months ago.

I was going to play the part, no one was going to take me back to where I had come from. I was on a roll with first class travel to America; we had all the treatment. I was never going back to baggage. I was being chaperoned by a billionaire. Nothing was expensive to Gino; it was just a bus ride to him. His take on it all was that it was all-tax deductible expenses, no one would be arguing with Gino at the tax office. He was totally geared up for low tax.

The guards were with us, checking out the people around us, just making sure there were no problems. I felt like I was in a protected bubble, everybody looking in at me, thinking *what's she doing there?* I felt safe. The guard's jacket was slightly open, and I could see a gun in a holster under the coat. I had read a lot about America, and it was a place to be careful in. You could never assume anything here. The guards were definitely needed; it wouldn't be safe for me and Gino here, well possibly I would be protecting Gino, as I had been bought up differently.

Gino had grown up in a western culture where I was fighting in the streets of Nigeria. Although I could look after myself, I was a tiger, I didn't want to be fighting off people in front of Gino. I think he would have collapsed in shame of me, ha, well, it was in my head. I had learned to trust nobody, my eyes were everywhere. We had a limousine waiting, and we all got into it. We were going downtown to Manhattan; this was where it would be taking place later in the year.

LA would be the first place for the fashion show, 13-15 March, only a few weeks away. I was really looking forward to LA and Hollywood, it was going to be an experience in front of all those successful dignitaries, film producers, actors, and fashion brands. It would be full; I had seen the show so many times on the internet. It was amazing the way it was all put together; I would have to step up.

I wanted to know that our models would have their own area; I wanted our show to be the best and not be copied by others. I had some good plans in my head for how it was going to be. I had no reason to discuss it with anybody, including Gino. I wanted to surprise him with some things I had planned in my head; it was all on the hard drive at the back of my head, and it would all be revealed later.

We were staying at a large colonial hotel; I have never heard about it, but Gino said he was always happy there. It had a certain feel about it. He felt comfortable there. We made our way there. It wasn't far away; I was ready for a sleep. Gino said he was hungry and ready for a nice meal and a bottle of wine. That was the last thing I wanted; forget the wine, I wasn't going to be drinking wine again. Enough was enough. I would have to get through this day; I was really tired, but I didn't want Gino to know. He had slept some of the way while I had been looking for contacts.

It seemed they were a bit thin on the ground. There weren't many takers for the diary entry. I had to be careful as Gino would twig. I didn't need him to find out I was doing overtime for myself in place of relaxing like Gino. He had been asleep; he must have been wacked out. He was a silent sleeper. It wouldn't have gone down well if he was sleeping like a bear, but he was a gentleman even when he was sleeping.

He was my hero; he had bought me to where I was now. I looked around the hotel; I wanted to run into the bathroom and scream with joy. I was here in the Waldorf Astoria; I was trying to pinch myself to see if I was awake and not dreaming. I was here in one of the best hotels in downtown Manhattan, New York. Surely it couldn't get better than this. It was a total dream in my eyes; there was nothing to compare with the luxury we had here.

CHAPTER 45

This was Gino's life; this was what he did every week and month: he would come over and see his biggest market for the clothes. He was a genius, *pinch me now I can't be this lucky.* The hotel was really busy, people all over the place. A butler came over and escorted us up to our rooms. He opened the door, there it was: the most beautiful grand piano in the middle of the floor. Unfortunately, I had the room across the hallway. The room was Gino's; I didn't know he played the piano.

We just had to settle Gino in; I nipped around the room as the butler hung up his clothes in the wardrobe. He was a king; they knew him. He was on first name terms with the butler. He must have spent a fortune on the room, and I couldn't wait to see mine. Gino was all done, and he was ready to go out for dinner, but I was excited to see my room. The butler asked if I was ready to approve the room.

"Yes, I'm ready," I replied.

"This way, madam," he said. It was the room was straight across from Gino's, which made things easier, though was probably too close for comfort. I wasn't looking forward to a knock on the door later or an invite over to his room. This was not what I was interested in anymore. I had grown up quickly, and I realised now any interaction with the boss was not a good thing, so it was never going to happen. Although it did cross my mind a lot, especially on trips away to these beautiful places.

The romance of it all was almost blooming, and I had now become a lady. I was just 18, but I felt like a grown woman with my own mind now. Nobody would be able to influence me any other way. I was going to keep my head down and stay away from trouble; affairs at work didn't work well. I had heard that a lot of relationships start at work, and this was not a good thing.

I wanted mine to be attraction, and I would love to get married properly to the man I love and not to someone I had an affair with. So, whilst Gino was there as a bird in the hand across the hallway, I was going to enjoy the time in New York sightseeing and being introduced to Gino's staff in the New York offices. I wanted to get straight on it, but the day was already over apart from going out for dinner.

The door opened and the butler escorted me in.

"This is your queen's room, madam." I looked up. Wow, what a fabulous place. The views were amazing, looking over all the skyscrapers of Manhattan, I could see the whole world, it seemed like. The bathroom was all part of the room with a large bath facing outside to the splendour of downtown Manhattan. I could see a park in the distance.

The butler said, "it's a nice view, madam. You can see Central Park in the distance."

That was it. I had heard about Central Park but never been there in America to see it. I wanted to ice skate in the winter on the lake; I could do it this Christmas coming. I knew we had a lot of fashion shows coming up, but I was sure I would be able to fit a couple of hours of skating. I would have to ask Gino his thoughts about dangerous sports whilst I was under contract to ensure I did my term for the company as the face of fashion.

I would have thought he would have tied me up, well, metaphorically, not in a physical way, but the contract would be far reaching with possibly sports like skating excluded. I had heard about these types of contracts and when you sign them you never know what you signed in the small print. Hey ho, we have to live for the moment. I probably wouldn't risk it, it wouldn't be worth the grief for me and Gino if anything happened. I would be in as much trouble as Gino.

I was just happy to be in this fabulous bedroom overlooking the park. I was going to have a bath later, after dinner. Gino had said we would have dinner here in the hotel as he said he had done every time he came here. It was too convenient on the first night, as we were tired due to the flight and transfers. I couldn't wait to get back up here and run that bath.

I went to the window and, as I looked into the bath, I could see it was a jacuzzi bath. I was so happy. I would be in it all night when I got back.

The butler said, "I can get the maid to come in and run you a bath, madam. Have you a time you would like us to run it?"

"Yes," I replied. "9pm would be just right, thank you." I looked around, but I could not see any blinds or curtains.

"Where are the blinds?" I asked the butler.

"Oh madam, there is no need for them. Only the birds can see up here, you will be fine, madam. If you have a problem, I could arrange a screen to be erected at the window,"

"No," madam Sazzar replied. "Let them have a show. I'm sure they will love what they see."

"Madam, you have made me blush."

"Oh, that's alright," madam Sazzar replied, "they won't have seen anything like me before."

"Yes madam," the butler said. "The birds will be falling out of the sky."

"Let them," she said. "They will have enjoyed the view."

"Yes, madam, I'm sure they would you're a beautiful woman."

"Thank you, that's so kind of you to say."

"You're welcome madam. Will you be requiring anything, else Madam Sazzar?"

Wow, he knew my name; I'm impressed, I thought.

"No that will be all," I replied. "Thank you."

The butler said, "madam, I'm on call so anything you want, just call." This is what I was born for; to be looked after. I wasn't born for hard work. I have left that behind me; this was now going to me for the rest of my life.

It seems a long time to be looked after like a queen, but I feel I was born in Africa. I was born to be a princess.

I needed this; wanting it would never be enough if you're having it. You need to decide if you want it or need it, everybody to their own, but I needed it and I was going to take it all. There would be no prisoners taken on my watch, it was a sink or swim scenario.

I could feel myself in that jacuzzi in all those bubbles looking out with a nice can of orange; no drinking alcohol was allowed in my regime. I was looking forward to relaxing, it was almost like heaven to be here, and it was all there for the taking. I was obviously working, having to meet people and talk about how we would be doing the fashion shows. It appeared I had said too much, done too much, and found myself talking myself into a load of work. That's my mouth opening and closing like a shutter door.

I had found my own work, but at least Gino could see I was more than value for money and that I earned my keep. I was not having to be told what to do by someone that had no real knowledge; at least I had fashion sense. I was so happy to be here, and I had no regrets. I was going to be here for the long haul, and it would never change. Gino looked like he had it all sewn up, but I had increased the amount of people appreciating the new catwalk and the accessories they carried now.

CHAPTER 46

I t had to have taken the ratings up to another level; I had enjoyed doing the work. I think Gino would be keeping me on after my probation work period. I was cruising. Gino had taken to me like a daughter; I was going nowhere. I was hungry and ready to eat, just waiting for the knock on the door. I was ready. *Great minds think alike*, I thought. as seconds later Gino knocked, and we went down for dinner.

It was a splendid place; it was like out of a film in the 20's. The butler had met us in the foyer near the restaurant; it was all a bit formal, but that's how it was with Gino. He was a celebrity, and he needed to be treated as one. This was what I would be looking for in my next years. Meeting here with the girls, having fun. Obviously I wouldn't be paying, and I wouldn't be entertaining any freeloaders or round dodgers.

They would all be with me for my company, and they would settle the bill accordingly. I was going to make sure I visited here regularly as I could smell the money here and I wanted it to be my place to cash in. I would definitely put it on the venue list of top places to meet rich people. I was hoping nobody would see me as a rich person, I had just a salary at the moment, but that would change to a large income in the next few years.

I was just finding my feet, and I would be parting on after that. I was enjoying Gino's company, he was a total gentleman. No one was going to spoil our relationship; we were a team, and I was going to play my part in it. I had it all covered for the next fashion show. It was going to be a different take on fashion; my mind was on overtime.

I was about to go into the plushest dining room ever, and I was thinking about work. I think I would have to revisit my position in the company as one of employees, not the director, I should be able to turn off when not working. I felt I was part of the family, and I wanted to do so well and change the way things were done. It seemed they were stuck in a time warp, and they were going backwards.

They needed fresh eyes to look at fashion and the new trends coming in and to look at what would sell and create sales at fashion shows. The fuddy duddy was out, and I had arrived to give a new fresh look on what international fashion was producing. I wanted to have a look at what Gino's fashion team were creating and how I could change the perception on what they were designing and bring them into the 21st century.

The way I saw it going, I was too much of a greenhorn to change anything here, but I could keep chipping away until I had turned the clothes into what I perceived as the fashion people all over the world would like and wear.

The butler escorted us into the dining room; it seemed strange the other people were all seated and here I was with the man being escorted to the table. I was so privileged to be in this company of a king; he was the king of fashion, and he commanded the best.

I felt a million dollars as the butler pulled out my chair to sit at the table. Gino, as usual, had seen somebody he knew and had turned to say hello to them. It was like being on stage, all the people at the tables were looking at us like they were the audience. All that was missing was the clapping. I was in my element. I could see people looking at my clothes and wondering who I was. Well, at last I was a celebrity in myself.

I was the international face of fashion on a salary that could top $500,000 a year, not too shabby for a girl from a working-class background. Gino was seated, and I looked at the menu. I thought it was rude to read the menu. If you were a couple, you read at the same time, that way you could discuss it with each other if we were sharing. I didn't think Gino would be seen sharing food with me, it was more of a couple type of thing. As for me, I had only shared food with my family never out.

I had been to a restaurant; it was only my second time in a public place eating out. We started off as usual, working from the outside to the centre. Gino was watching me, I think just to see if I needed help. He wasn't a man to interfere where he wasn't needed. I was loving the service; it was strange that I could have been doing a job like that in Africa or anywhere else.

I had seen the potential in myself, so I would be going for it to do the best. Who would have believed how far you can go with very little capital or experience? I kept thinking about that jacuzzi and getting in it, but the first course was on its way and I had to order my main course. I was uncertain. I had prawn cocktail for my starter followed by, well, I wasn't sure. It was a tossup between braised beef and seasonal vegetables with glazed gravy or the fish of the day.

I was already having fish in the prawns, so I opted for the special, the braised beef. Gino was having the steak off the menu, so we were both on the beef. We had a good chat about how he wanted to move forward and try and get me more involved with the business like a consultant in fashion. He now believed I had a talent besides a beautiful body; I was more than a pretty face. I had a talent for fashion, and he wanted me to use it.

We would be having further conversations on this later, but we were both ready to go and chill out. I couldn't wait to get up to my room. The butler said the maid would fill the jacuzzi by nine pm, and it was 9pm now, so I wanted to get straight into it. I walked up the stairs for a change, just for some exercise. Gino took the lift as we said good night. It had been a long day, and I just needed a soak. I got undressed straight away; I needed that bath more than anything.

I got in, it was heaven, so lovely I could feel the bubbles all over me alerting my senses. It was so good; I was looking out the window, which was floor to ceiling. I thought, *could anybody see me on a plane or a helicopter?* I wasn't going to give a view of my body for nothing; this would have to be paid for. I wasn't a glamour model; I was the face of fashion, and I was not cheap to hire for modelling.

I thought to myself *let me stand up and see if anyone below could see me,* so I stood up and leaned forward onto the window. *I hope it's safe to lean on,* I thought. I heard a knock on the door.

"Come in," I shouted. *The maid must be here to see how I'm doing.* The door opened, and I looked behind me. There was Gino.

"My God," I cried. I had my back to him; everything was on show. I didn't turn round, as he would have had a shock.

CHAPTER 47

I didn't know what to do. As I turned my head around to answer Gino, he had turned away, and he apologised for walking in.

I said, "oh it's okay, it's not a problem. I thought it was the maid."

Wow, I thought, *he must have seen me bending over to look down, he must have seen everything, but he was too shy to say anything.* Being a model, girls are always getting changed with an audience around them, but he had a full eyeful of me before he turned around. My fault for not locking the door.

I hope I had put his heartrate up; he would definitely have something to think about tonight. That was his sleep ruined for the night; I wonder what he thought. It would have taken a great photo; he was a gentleman, he was not going to stop and stare at me. We were friends, and I was an employee, and it was not going beyond that.

Although he had seen it all before, he hadn't seen me with nothing on.

It was all my fault, and I would apologise in the morning; I was that desperate to get into that jacuzzi I forgot to lock the door. I was like a little girl wanting something so bad. I had never seen a jacuzzi never mind gone in one. I relaxed until the water went cold; it was like I had gone to heaven and back. I was so impressed by it. I hope nobody saw me at the window, they would have definitely got a free shot.

I was opening up more to my sexuality. I was a grown woman, and everything was there for the taking, obviously with my permission. I had been a bit naughty during the time in the jacuzzi, I blame it on the bubbles, as they seemed to excite my senses, and I had a really good time. I was overexcited; I was enjoying myself until the water went cold. I needed to exit the bath; I needed to get some sleep. I was burning the candle too much; I needed to get back to my African routine of bed early, up late.

I had to get my 12 hours sleep if I could make it. I was doing 8 hours, but I needed 12 like every busy lady does. I was in bed ready, for sleep. I had to say my prayers as I do every night. I'm sure someone up there was looking after me. I would not be having anybody next to me for two years at least. I could get by without a man, I had to in Africa, as I was underage, so I would have been in big trouble if I had come home pregnant.

I couldn't afford to take the risk, and it paid off as I still have a great figure and I'm as free as a bird ready to spread my wings and discover what's out there waiting for me. It was so exciting. Every day was another experience; I was in my favourite place, America. Everything happened here, it was a great place to be, especially as I was young and wanted to take it all in.

Everything I dreamed about was here. This was the land of milk and honey, and I was here to milk it all. Honestly, I never worked outside the law, everything I did would be legal. I had never been in trouble, and I wasn't going to start now. Tomorrow would be another day; I looked forward to every day. I woke up. It was hopefully going to be a blessed day.

I had found my feet here with Gino, I laughed a little about how he was when he saw me nude. I was so happy it was him and not the butler, now that would have been a different scenario. I trusted Gino. Although he was a shy man, he was brilliant and could always get out of a situation like tonight. I'm sure he might be embarrassed tomorrow at breakfast, but he is a man of the world so he should recover fast.

Thinking about it, I sniggered to myself; it must have been a shock when he opened the door and saw me bending over the jacuzzi to look at the ground outside, showing all my bits and pieces. I think he was more embarrassed than me, well it would soon be morning and the start of another day. I could only hope for the best for both of us; he was in my prayers.

It was morning. I must have dropped straight off; I always slept fast, as I had nothing much on my mind. There was nothing much going off in my head, but once I was awake it was buzzing ready for whatever the day threw at me. The morning came fast; I was still tired, but I knew Gino would be there early so I had to move my lazy bones and get sorted out. I had my shower; I looked over at the jacuzzi, which was calling me to come in.

I wish I could have run a bath and got in it for the day then gone to bed and sleep my head off. It was criminal to expect anybody to get up before 11am. What on earth was Gino trying to do to me? I would not be able to cope with early mornings. I'm sure he may have been able to make some exceptions for me, but then again why would he? I was an employee, not a boss but

I supposed I would have to get used to it until I was my own boss.

There he was, 8am the knock on the door from the butler.

"Excuse me, Madam, the boss is in the breakfast room today. It looks over the city. I've put you right next to the window."

"Oh, thank you, I will be two minutes."

"Okay madam," the butler said. "I will wait." Well, that was a nightmare to have him standing outside; it was only an estimated time. 10 minutes later, I was coming out the door.

"Excuse me, sorry, it's a woman thing; we always need a bit more time. We have a lot more to look after."

"Oh, I understand, madam. I will escort you to the breakfast room. Are you hungry, madam?"

"Yes, you could say that, but I have to look after my figure."

"Yes, I can see you're in good shape," the butler said.

"Yes, I do regulate it by diet."

"That's so good to be healthy," the butler replied.

"Yes, I've always been this way."

The butler went in front and said, "it's only on the top floor; it's been done recently just to make breakfast a little more interesting. It's nice to dine in a nice room. I think they did a fabulous job on the conversion."

"It's very nice," I said as I got to the door.

"Yes, madam, it was a big job, but it's paid off; we have a lovely room. The boss is over at the window in the corner; he likes that seat." *Likes that seat* – they even knew what seat in the dining room he liked, and it was reserved for him. He was a king here, but his room rate price would have choked a donkey. It would have been thousands a night but we had come on business so he could claim it all back.

It was all on the expenses, but it was a fortune to me gone in a night at a hotel. I could have lived three years in Africa. I sat down at the table and the butler served us both. Gino had been sitting there all that time waiting for me to come down. I apologised. He said he was just having some time for thought, and he was okay to wait; he had been drinking his morning coffee so he was chilling.

The butler asked, "are you ready, sir, madam, for your breakfast?"

I jumped in without looking. "Yes, I'm starving."

Gino smiled. I think he was looking at me as if to say *well, you should get up earlier,* but I was not used to late nights and early mornings. I liked to relax, get up late, and give myself time to wake up; Gino was a bit like a regimented Sargent major – everything had to be perfect. I was always one to look my best. I always felt better dressed to go anywhere. That way I was never caught out looking untidy.

I always needed to know I was stepping up and looking good. People do actually judge you on your appearance. Gino had already complimented me on my style of clothes and how beautiful I looked. I was beginning to accept I was his daughter now and not his lover. Everything was happening for a reason. I had to be clear of any scandal; I could not afford to be in any divorce courts cited as the reason. I could only be myself, a single person ready to mingle, but my common sense overruled my whim to go the extra mile and remove my virgin status with some one-night love affair and, worse, get pregnant.

Gino was sitting there, eating his breakfast. He had no idea at all what was going through my head. I was a woman, and I had all the traits of one. I was always thinking and always looking for new horizons, things to discover, or openings to be explored. I was definitely a woman. If Gino only knew what a lucky escape he had

had… It was unreal. If he really knew what a nightmare was, he hadn't met me yet as the nightmare, but I would be trying to supress myself as Gino was the boss, not my boyfriend.

I would respect every decision he made; he was my boss, and he was paying me, so I had to make sure that I followed protocol. He was the boss, I was the employee; he could replace me, but not that easily. Where would he get someone to replace me? I was underestimating myself. I had turned a boring fashion show into something that was now going to change catwalk fashion forever. Everyone that was someone saw the change in International Fashion's catwalk, and they all loved it, but Gino took the credit from me.

I was all okay with that, but he didn't give me a bonus on his sales he made through my efforts. Still, I enjoyed what I did, and Gino had given his trust to take it all on. I was thrown in the deep end, but I work well under pressure as long as I'm in control of what I'm responsible for. I would always give him my best, as I saw him as a best friend as well as my employer, but I was his top woman, so it worked both ways.

CHAPTER 48

He had a really good disposition about him; he was always chilled out. I never heard him raise his voice. It was a good job I had landed, and I had the best employer anyone could have asked for. He was a pleasure to work for. Everything about him made you do the best you could for him. I was so lucky to have met him. We were going to his offices and outlets in the city; I was excited to be seeing the Manhattan area I had heard so much about.

All the fashion shops I wanted to be feasting my eyes on, all the fashion trends, and what was so different to what Gino's designers were turning out. If I could just get to look at the styles of clothing, it would give me a good idea where we would be going in the next two years. I had set myself up to do my best with the tools I had, which were me and my ideas for fashion.

I wanted to be the leader in ladies' and men's fashion for the autumn collection. I knew I could pull off the best fashion show ever. I wanted to make Gino proud of the day he met me. I had to pull it off.

The drivers came into the hotel, and we were ready to go to the offices and design centre. This was where people worked on the new designs for the autumn collection. I wanted to see what they were working on and see what my thoughts were. After all, they had to be clothes we could wear.

There could be nothing worse than seeing models struggling to walk in their outfits. The more comfortable the model, the better the feeling for her to show off the clothing. They can swagger in place of looking for their steps in case they fall in some awkward outfit. My advice would be to go with my ideas. Fashion shows sell clothes, and if someone is wearing something too big, it's a statement the models won't feel good in them, and it will transfer the awkwardness from the model to the audience.

If it flows, the audience moves with it. I had some really good ideas of how I wanted to see the industry in two years' time. Hopefully, it would have moved forward if I could bring my way of thinking into the business. I'm sure Gino would be seeing his profits moving up in the right direction. As long as I could show him results, he would have faith in me and leave me to expand my mind and create a whole new take on fashion.

My thoughts were running wild, and I knew it would be a risk to take on board what I was thinking. It was a multibillion-dollar company at the height of fashion. Here was a young girl from Africa trying to give my take on how it should be run. The problem as I see it was that would I have the confidence that Gino would expect me to have. For saying I might want to change possibly the whole collection, I was thinking negatively, and I was a positive person.

I was going to change it or struggle to get the right image of the new fashion over to the buyers and press and the guests. I had waited my whole short life for this opportunity; I did not want to be a designer reinventing the wheel. All my designs were new and not seen in any fashion shows anywhere in the world. I was at the top of my career, but nobody had ever noticed me besides Gino.

I wasn't in a good place in Africa, but things were now changing. I was now in my favourite place in the world, I was in my element here, and I was buzzing with excitement. I had never seen anywhere like where I was now, it was somehow magical in its entirety. It held some kind of spell over me; I was transfixed into the fabric of everything I could see. I was looking out the car window at the people walking by us on the way to work. We were not going anywhere walking; Gino had said always travel by car in big cities, as you were safer and the fumes were better in the vehicle than outside walking.

The air quality was not good, and the security could not be guaranteed. Gino had pointed out that I was a celebrity and I would not have the same freedom to walk around like before. All that would change now, as Madam Sazzar had become a target for criminals' gangs. We were under the spotlight and needed to be careful where we went on our own. We needed security to move freely around; my life would never be the same again.

It seemed the norm to have security; I was used to being as free as a bird, but I could not be exposed to any danger. Gino had it all sorted. I was never going to be out there vulnerable, although I was a tiger, and I could only defend myself on a one-to-one basis. We had arrived at a really tall building and there were men on the door of the building who came to the car as we stopped.

The man opened the door.

"Nice to see you back, sir," one of the men said.

"Yes," Gino said, "it's always nice to see you." We exited the car into the foyer of this monster building.

I said to Gino, "is this all yours?"

"No," he replied. "We're on the top floors."

"Wow, the views must be stunning."

"Well, yes, when you have the time to look, they're fabulous. You can see most of the city. It has a full panoramic view."

"I can't wait to see them," I said.

"Yes, I think you will like them," Gino replied.

The door opened from the lift. I could feel my legs, and I nearly collapsed when I saw the view. I had never seen anything so stunning; I could see the other end of the world; the views went that far. I went to every window to look out; the views were fabulous everywhere you looked. This was so the place to be, to have an office here was a dream. How big was Gino's empire? It seemed to be endless; there were another three floors below us. I couldn't think about the cost of running the empire he had created.

No wonder the price of clothes and bags was high: it was all overheads that you needed to pay before you even started making money.

CHAPTER 49

Gino had taught me something. I wouldn't be going into manufacturing clothes, bags, and accessories – that was way too far out of my reach. Even when I was receiving my money, it wouldn't pay the rent on a table in this place, which was a money pit swallowing up money to make money. I could see how it all worked; you had to have money to make money.

It would not be any use trying to do anything until I had some backers. I had heard of too many businesses going to the wall through lack of funding from the banks. Gino said they were just there for themselves and didn't care a hoot if you sank or swam. I had gained so much knowledge from Gino in such a sort time, and he admitted he had been learning a lot from me.

He had asked me if I went to grammar school.

"Oh, yes," I replied, fingers crossed behind my back. I never went to any school, what I learned was in the streets near my house. How had I been able to keep my virginity there with all the street lads after me? I think they knew not to make the approach; it would have been a deadly move. I took no prisoners; they would get what was coming to them, and I wasn't going to be good. I packed a punch to knock a donkey down, no one stood a chance when they got a right hook from me. Although it was rare, when it came, it was fierce, and men and women would fall at the side of me if the fists came out.

I think they had all heard about me, and they kept their distance. The one that would eventually catch me would be the obscure one that nobody knew. I was up for anything. *Bring it on,* I used to say; it turned people around to walk the other way. They had met the tyrant -- what a dangerous move for the fainthearted to meet a monster. That's what they said on the streets: they called me a monster. Not the best compliment a girl could receive, but nobody asked why people called me the monster.

When I had finished fighting, I had extracted my fair share of blood. They never came back for more; enough was enough. I was nobody's fool; I made sure I made my mark if someone came to upset my day. Putting that aside, it was time to go and have a look at the fashion shows below on the 81st floor. The 1st floor was reserved for conferencing and fashion shows; there would be a good turnout. He was saying I was desperate to look at how different theirs was compared with mine.

I was hoping it was not going to come up to scratch, it would have to run its course. It was not my baby; it was their job to make sure it worked, and everything was as it should be. There were going to be a lot of people buying, and Gino needed to create a proper fashion show. This wasn't Milan, this was New York: the biggest fashion clothing industry in the world. If we didn't make it here, we would be in trouble for the rest of the year and orders would be poor.

My head was racing. I could see I might have to go down and take over; we couldn't afford to pull off a bad show. It would have looked so poor on the company; Gino would have to put his faith in me again. I was going to have to take over; I was going to meet some fireworks here in America. I don't think I would be welcome, but if they didn't like it, they knew where the door is. I think Gino liked me taking over; he seemed to revel in my ruthless ways.

I sorted the staff out, but I could not see Gino have a bad show. They needed me behind them; I could see that there was no organisation and everybody was waiting around. There was no order, and they were walking around like headless chickens. There was no organisation. I turned to Gino.

"Would you like me to sort all this out?"

"Be my guest, Madam Sazzar." In an instant, Gino told the manager Madam Sazzar was now in control of the show.

I watched their faces drop to the ground, wondering *who the hell is she?* Well, that's what would have come out if they couldn't hold it in. I could see the hate in them; *what does this idiot know about catwalk? she is only just out the pram, and she is telling us what to do.* They sat down in some kind of protest. That was okay for Madam Sazzar, she needed to see the full collection and match the right outfit to the right model.

I looked over. Gino was sitting down, having a coffee with his feet up. He was leaving it all to me. I wasn't going to let him down; I would be walking them all out to show them all how it had to be done. Gino had a piece of cake. He was in his element, sitting back. He had bought the fox in to sort out the chickens; there was a lot of settling needed in the henhouse. It appeared more or less the same as the Milan models.

I would soon nip these into place. I looked back over at Gino again; he was smiling about something. He was chilling big-time, feet up; he had only just got out of bed, and he has his feet up. I laughed to myself. *Let's get it all started; we have four hours to go to the show, so I have to get kicking a few into shape.* I wanted to make sure they were all aware who the boss was.

I was taking no rubbish back from them, they would have to put up or shut up. They would have no quarrel with me. I was in it for the long haul until I moved into different circles and was exactly where I wanted to be. I would not miss out on my social circles, but I was here now, in control of the catwalk shows. Gino had indicated that he wanted me now to choreograph all the catwalks and for me to do absolutely everything.

I was hoping for a high rise in my wages. I was more now than just the face of fashion, I was the right-hand girl. I was not about to give up my spare time for anything but money; that was my driver, and I wanted to be driven big time financially. Forget the fame that goes fast, the money tends to stay longer. The face of fashion 24/25, who will remember that? Probably just Gino, he would hopefully be financially better off for meeting me.

I would just have to work hard to get everything working tickety-boo. It was easy for me. I'd had 18 years of getting ready for this job; I was born to be in fashion.

CHAPTER 50

I would be focused now on moving the models into place and deciding who was wearing what. They would have to dress themselves; I had no time to fuss about after them. There seemed to be a lot of clothes. It was going to be a long show, and I had my work cut out. I would have to make sure we were carrying no dead wood, that was just here for the money.

They had to go the extra mile for me, or they would never to return. This wasn't school, it was reality: sink or swim. I was looking for good swimmers and the ones that could not hack it would sink out of sight of International Fashion. I was on it now, we had less than four hours, so we had to move quickly, or they would be going out in their lingerie without the clothes.

I wanted top marks for this show; nothing was going to hold me back, and the models and staff needed to be behind me if we were going to pull this off. We couldn't afford to lose the momentum; we would never get it back.

People remembered bad shows rather than the good ones. This was going to knock them out, it would be the best fashion show ever. Everybody in fashion would be talking about it for a long time. It was in my head, and all I had to do was put it into action and get the result I wanted.

I was proactive in what I did and only wanted the best. If it wasn't the best, I didn't want it. I was going to sort out the clothes while makeup were doing the models' faces. I was going to sort out the format in which they would be cat-walking; it would have to be so good. I was looking through the curtain. The press were setting up, there were that many cameras I wasn't sure where the dignitaries and buyers were going to sit.

They seemed to have taken over, but I was assured by the organisers there would be plenty of room when the cameras were in position. *Okay,* I thought, *I hope so.* I wasn't aware if it was going to be televised. It would be going all over the world; I could feel my palms and forehead starting to sweat. Millions of people, could be beyond a billion people, watching my show. I was in pieces, but I could do it. Nothing was impossible, it just took a bit longer.

I was looking cool, but my heart was racing faster than a Formula One car. I had to make it work;

everything was going well. The saucepan was boiling. I just couldn't wait until it was simmering that would indicate I had it all under control and on time. Things were coming together. Some of the girls were fighting to wear certain clothes. I soon sorted that out and told them I was going to be selecting what clothes they were going to be wearing.

We didn't want any larger women trying to make a silk purse out of a pig's ear. We needed all the models to make the clothes look as good as they could. I wasn't prepared to be bullied into submission to people that had no idea. I was in total control and that's the way it was going to stay. *Do they ever learn?* was in my thoughts, *they all must be stupid.* They must have been told about me.

We were good to go; all the models had the right lingerie on that wouldn't show under the clothes. All I had to do is start dishing out the clothes, and I had plenty of stock. I had a great eye for fashion, so I always had the right clothes picked out for the right models. This was the show. It had to be the best ever, there could be no mistakes. I was the lead so it would be following my lead -- that's all they had to do. I would have my eye on them as they came down the catwalk.

It was going to be looking good and keeping everybody looking at the clothes. They were all dressed now, all looking fabulous. Just a bit of a tidy up with the clothes, and they were ready to go out. All they needed was a smoke, most of the girls had a cigarette, and we were ready. I was looking through the curtain. It was full to the brim; everyone was seated, ready to go.

I had put another routine, every walk and the finish had to be defined so I would be the first to stop halfway through the catwalk, and we would all stop one behind the other. When the last one had joined, I wanted us to all turn together to the left then to the right and then turn into the middle, taking a bow to the crowd. We started the walk; it was intense coming out from behind the curtain to a rapturous applause.

Everybody started off walking out from behind the curtain, and they followed me. I only hoped my friends, sisters and family were watching on TV; it was on live shows on all social media channels. It was the spring/summer fashion, and it was going well. Everything was how it should be: the girls were doing so well, they were actually smiling. We got to bunch together at the end, and we turned left and then right and to the middle and bowed our heads.

The whole room went up in a rapturous applause. Everyone stood up clapping – even some of the press were clapping. I had pulled off the impossible, and we were all reaping the reward of our work. We got behind the curtain to an audience still clapping, it was so good. I went to the back. Gino was outside somewhere taking down numbers for clothing sales.

He came into the back room five minutes later.

"Well done, Madam Sazzar," he said. "What a stunning performance, never ever seen one like that in my whole life. Take any clothes or bags you want, you have earned them."

"Thank you," Madam Sazzar said to Gino.

"My pleasure," he said. The clothes were all high fashion brands, and I was going to have a pick of all of them. I would give some pieces to the models, but I needed to stock up on my cloths. I was in for everything. Just whilst I was packing away the clothes, I could see a well-groomed gentleman walking towards me.

It was definitely me he wanted; he looked really nice a tad too old but amazingly attractive. He had my attention. Whatever he was selling, I was buying.

"Madam Sazzar," he spoke very softly.

"Yes," I replied, "That's me, how can I help you, sir?"

"Well," he replied, "I know you, but you don't know me. I'm Gino's stepbrother. I am also in fashion, in fact, Gino and I are partners in some companies, but we trade independently. I have my own fashion houses, and I've never come across anybody like you. The shows you put on were splendid. I have never seen such professionalism ever in my time of being in fashion.

"Pardon me, I haven't introduced myself properly. I thought you should know what the connection was between myself and Gino. I know you have a very good rapport going with Gino and he is a really good man, but I always feel I am more proactive in my approach to fashion. I want you to consider working for me. I'm Renaldo Latimore of World Fashion Inc. I just want you to put in your ideas. You would have total control over all the fashion shows and an input on our latest collections. You would have a two-year contract with an option to renew for another two years, and a golden parachute indexed linked pension."

What was that? I had never heard of a pension. I would have to check it out later. Gino had never mentioned it. What was this golden parachute? He had me thinking. He gave me his card and said, "ring me and we can talk more about my proposal."

"Oh yes," Madam Sazzar replied, "I will, definitely." I needed to be able to sort out what the points he was making.

As he was leaving, he said, "it's a one-off offer. You can write your own cheque, that's how much I want us to work together."

I was a bit in the dark, as I was not aware of this terminology. I needed to do some research on this brother of Gino's. I wouldn't like to tell him I thought this would be counterproductive as I had the best job ever already. Gino had been so good to me ever since I met him that day. He changed my life. I had a debt of gratitude to pay back to him; he had been a lifesaver.

I don't know where I would have been if it wasn't for him giving me a lift. If I left, it would be like stabbing him in the back. I couldn't do it to him, but I had to look after myself. I always said I was available to the highest bidder; I was here now, having to make a decision to go or stay. The money was staring me in the face; *write your own cheque. I could put double what I'm getting now.* I would have to work two years to get what I would get with World Fashion. I would have to think what I came to Europe for. Was it to make a friend or money?